"You Can't Change What Happened Here This Morning,"

Joshua said quietly. "You are mine. I am yours. We'll face your past. Whatever it is."

"I'm afraid," Leigh confessed. His hands held her securely to the warmth of his body. And still she feared.

"I'll be there. I promise."

Her eyes searched his. He was offering her all that she had thought lost. Was she brave enough to take a chance? "Does it have to be now? I need time," she pleaded finally.

Joshua wanted to refuse. Yet he couldn't make himself force her.

"All right. Take your time. But don't shut me out. I'm here, and here is where I'm staying—no matter what you do...."

Dear Reader:

Series and Spin-offs! Connecting characters and intriguing interconnections to make your head whirl.

In Joan Hohl's successful trilogy for Silhouette Desire— *Texas Gold* (7/86), *California Copper* (10/86), *Nevada Silver* (1/87)—Joan created a cast of characters that just wouldn't quit. You figure out how *Lady Ice* (5/87) connects. And in August, "J.B." demanded his own story—*One Tough Hombre*. In *Falcon's Flight*, coming in November, you'll learn *all* about . . .?

Annette Broadrick's *Return to Yesterday* (6/87) introduced Adam St. Clair. This August *Adam's Story* tells about the woman who saves his life—and teaches him a thing or two about love!

The six Branigan brothers appeared in Leslie Davis Guccione's *Bittersweet Harvest* (10/86) and *Still Waters* (5/87). September brings *Something in Common*, where the eldest of the strapping Irishmen finds love in unexpected places.

Midnight Rambler by Linda Barlow is in October—a special Halloween surprise, and totally unconnected to anything.

Keep an eye out for other Silhouette Desire favorites— Diana Palmer, Dixie Browning, Ann Major and Elizabeth Lowell, to name a few. You never know when secondary characters will insist on their own story. . . .

All the best,

Isabel Swift
Senior Editor & Editorial Coordinator
Silhouette Books

SARA CHANCE
Double Solitaire

Silhouette Desire

Published by Silhouette Books New York

America's Publisher of Contemporary Romance

SILHOUETTE BOOKS
300 East 42nd St., New York, N.Y. 10017

Copyright © 1987 by Sydney Ann Clary

ISBN: 0-373-05388-6

First Silhouette Books printing November 1987

America's Publisher of Contemporary Romance

Printed in the U.S.A.

SARA CHANCE,

"wife, mother, author in that order," currently resides in Florida with her husband. With the ocean minutes from her door, Ms. Chance enjoys both swimming and boating.

To Cindy with my thanks,
for being a believer and helping me be a believer too.

One

"This road's a killer, Dutch," Leigh Mason muttered, glancing at the handsome wolflike dog occupying the passenger seat, while maneuvering the charcoal-gray pickup around another twisting turn.

Dusk cast deceptive shadows over the rural Tennessee countryside, increasing the loneliness of the deserted highway snaking over the hilly terrain. It had been a long two days picking up crafts for her store from the suppliers. Now she was on the way home, her truck fully loaded with new merchandise.

"It's times like these when I wish you were human, my friend."

The keeshond was Leigh's constant companion and, on buying trips like these, her protector. Not that she'd ever had any trouble. But habits learned in a lifetime of growing up and working in Chicago before she'd moved to Knoxville had made her cautious. Thinking about her hometown reminded her of her best friend, Jean, and the letter she had received this morning. The news it'd contained had been startling and most unwelcome. Over the years she had gotten used to an occasional reference to her ex-husband, Buddy, and later to his wife. But this time Jean's note had announced that Buddy was now divorced and, more importantly, had been asking about her.

For a moment Leigh's gray eyes darkened at the memory of the life she'd left behind, and the accident that had turned her dream into a nightmare. The future had held such promise until that afternoon long ago. She could still hear the scream of brakes, metal tearing at metal and then unearthly silence.

"Breaker! Breaker! This is an emergency! Is there a highway patrolman listening?"

Startled at the frantic CB message intruding into the silence of the cab, Leigh jerked out of the mists of the past and swore softly. She didn't often let herself dwell on what couldn't be changed. Life was too short for that kind of stupidity.

"Breaker! Breaker! Is there anyone there?"

Leigh frowned at the note of panic in the unknown woman's voice. The caller sounded close to the breaking point. Tension licked along Leigh's spine as she waited for the plea to be answered. She started to reach for the microphone, then hesitated. The woman was asking for a law-enforcement officer. Maybe it would be better not to interfere.

"Besides it could be a trick," she added under her breath while scanning the road ahead. From the clarity of the radio transmission she knew whoever it was had to be nearby.

"Please, someone answer. I'm in a runaway camper. The brakes are gone. I'm pregnant. My husband can't hold the truck on the road." The staccato sentences were ragged, fright and despair underlying each syllable.

I'm pregnant. The words flashed in Leigh's mind, destroying any other consideration. Snatching the mike, she keyed it with one hand and guided her now accelerating truck with the other.

"Breaker for the runaway. What's your position?"

"Oh heavens, I don't know."

"Describe the land around you," Leigh commanded swiftly, straining to pick out even a hint of the vehicle ahead.

"We just passed a deserted barn on the right. The road's curving away from the stream on the same side, but there is a drop-off on the left and it's getting steeper."

Frowning, Leigh ran the tortuous route through her mind. Vaguely she was glad she traveled this stretch so often. It made the task of locating the distressed party easier.

"I think you're about two miles in front of me," she announced finally. "Now listen. I've got a dark gray pickup with a shell on the back. I should catch up with you in a few minutes so watch for me. When you see me, get as far to the right as you can and hold it there. I'll pass you.''

"Why?''

"To stop you. We're going to use my brakes to do it,'' Leigh stated with more assurance than she felt.

She certainly hoped her old friend and supplier, Pop, hadn't been spinning her a yarn about how he had once done what she was about to attempt. She released the mike button to fumble in the compartment for the voice-activated CB headset that had been her assistant's Christmas gift last year. For once she was glad of Sally's originality, which had prompted her to purchase the lightweight, operator-style harness.

"I hope I can pull this off,'' Leigh mumbled.

Topping the next rise, Leigh caught sight of the white camper careening across the road. The swaying vehicle slid in wide arcs over both lanes of the highway, making her stomach clench in fear and determination. The worst part of the highway was coming up. What if she couldn't do it? If ever there was a long shot, this was it. The sheer drop on the left was an unforgiving landing spot. She had nothing left to lose, but those people ahead did. Her face set in a do-or-die expression, she sent the pickup hurtling after the runaway.

"Okay, I'm coming up on your tail. Ease it over.'' The second the vehicle hugged the right she shot past it with a roar of the double-barreled carbs. "I'm slowing down now. Line up with my bumper. It's heavy-duty so don't worry. The first few cracks will be the hardest. After that they'll come closer together until we stick. All you have to do is make sure you hit straight on. *Don't shear off!* Any questions?" Leigh waited a moment, then continued. "Are you ready?"

For a fleeting instant Leigh wondered why she wasn't nervous or, worse yet, paralyzed with terror. Not that she'd had the time for either emotion, she decided a moment later. She was too busy praying, holding on to her nerve and keeping the truck straight on the road.

"Ready." The quavery response was unsure enough for all of them.

"Let's do it!"

Within seconds the first contact snapped Leigh forward hard against the seat belt. Dutch whined while he scrambled for balance on the floor of the truck. Another crash—a moment to recover—then again—recover—again until the bumpers fused together by the equality of the speed of both trucks.

"Now what?" the unknown woman demanded.

"Now we get you stopped. Just hold it straight," Leigh commanded grimly, feeling the push from the bulky weight behind.

"A light touch," she prompted herself. "Slow and easy. Brake a little. Let up a touch. A bit more. Don't burn 'em up. Lightly! Don't let 'em buck. Watch the speedometer. It's dropping! Don't get cocky. You're not home yet. That's it. A little more—more—forty—thirty—twenty—fifteen—five—I did it!"

A smile, swiftly turning into a grin of pure delight at her success, lit Leigh's face. "Ease it to the right with me."

"Yes, yes," the woman agreed fervently.

Finally Leigh stopped the two trucks on the shoulder of the road and breathed a deep sigh of relief. Unclasping her fingers from the steering wheel, she stared at the white marks her death grip had etched in them. For a minute she savored the return of feeling.

"We did it, Dutch. We actually did it," Leigh said, her smoky voice losing the crisp sharpness the emergency had lent it. After unfastening her seat belt she slid out of the truck to check on the couple she had rescued. Studiously avoiding a look at the sheer drop across the highway, she approached the camper. Expecting an expression of relief to match her own, she was shocked to discover a distraught woman curled uncomfortably on the seat, her husband bent anxiously over her.

"What's wrong?" Leigh asked sharply, easing the door on the passenger side open.

The man lifted his head, barely focusing on her face before his gaze returned to his wife. "She's cramping. Oh God! It's the baby! I tried not to bump her around. I swear I did."

Leigh studied the pain-etched features of the woman, never feeling more helpless in her life. The victim needed a hospital, and the closest one was a good twenty miles away. The past merged with the present, tightening her nerves. Forcing herself to concentrate only on this woman, this accident, Leigh tried to think. She was all they had. Regardless of how she felt, she had to hold herself together.

"Hang in there, honey," she murmured, pushing back the young woman's dark, damp curls with an unsteady hand. "We'll get you to help." She glanced up to find the man's eyes fastened on her, a desperate plea in the worried depths. "I'll be right back."

Moving quickly, she shoved a rock under each of the camper's four wheels. Then she drove her pickup forward enough to let the tailgate down and the shell door up. Shifting the boxes of handcrafted goods she had collected to one side, Leigh made room for the woman and her husband. Between Leigh and the man, they transferred the woman to the bed of the truck and made her comfortable. Then they were on the road again, the pickup roaring into the early evening dusk like a modern-day, dark-winged angel of mercy.

The pass-through window between the cab and the back was open, allowing Leigh to hear the young man trying to calm his wife. Thinking to help herself as well as them, Leigh asked about their destination.

Once started, the words tumbled from them both. The house they had bought in Knoxville, the moving they had to do, and the new job. Details that really meant little now. Leigh listened, finding that the nervous conversation kept her mind occupied while she concentrated on holding the speeding truck on the road.

"I'm so scared, Ray," the woman cried tearfully.

He pushed back the damp hair from his wife's forehead. "I know, Missy. It's all my fault. If only I hadn't been so determined to take this damn trip. I should have listened to Joshua.'' Ray's self-recrimination was harsh and swift.

"No. I won't have you saying that." Tears rolled down Missy's cheeks as she tried to comfort her husband. "I wanted to come just as much as you did. Even Josh had to admit that in the end. You know he did."

The couple held hands tightly, drawing strength from each other. Leigh caught the look they exchanged in the rearview mirror, feeling a flash of envy so intense it startled her. Once she would have given anything to have had her husband by her side supporting her the way Missy's was doing. But Buddy hadn't been there when she needed him most. Far from it. He had left her and the situation that he could not handle. The dark memory threatened to overwhelm her. Leigh pushed it back, knowing she couldn't afford to lose one moment of concentration.

"Who is Joshua?" she asked, more to divert herself than her passengers.

"Missy's brother," Ray replied, sparing Leigh a quick look before he glanced out the window. "Are we nearly there?"

"Just another few minutes," Leigh replied, noting the landmarks. "Hang in there, you two. We'll make it."

The pair in the back said nothing as another pain gripped Missy and she cried out. Ray held her hand, his face as contorted as his wife's. "As soon as we get to the hospital I'll call Josh, honey," he whispered hoarsely.

"All I need is you," Missy gasped out.

Ray's expression lightened marginally at her words. "You'll have us both. He loves you, and he wouldn't forgive me if I didn't call him."

There was barely time for Missy to acknowledge Ray's reply with a nod before Leigh shot into the emergency area of Maryville Hospital. She was never more glad to see anything in her life. Missy's groans, though partially suppressed, were worrying her. She knew only too well how dangerous the first trimester of a pregnancy could be. Scarcely allowing the truck to roll to a stop, Leigh jumped out and ran to the back of the shell. Alerted by their tire-screaming and horn-blaring arrival, the hospital staff raced out of the emergency-room doors.

"Come in with me, please," Ray pleaded as the nurses and orderlies placed Missy on the stretcher.

Leigh caught the hand the younger man extended, out of sheer reflex. "If you like," she agreed. She couldn't help but admire the strength and courage he had shown in the crisis. He had been as frightened as his wife, yet he had come through when Missy had needed him.

"Would you like me to get in touch with Missy's brother while you wait for the doctor?" She had no idea what made her offer. The last place she wanted to spend any time was in a hospital, regardless of the circumstances. But she couldn't let this gallant couple down.

"Would you?" For a split second, a flicker of relief dispelled the worry in his eyes. Digging in his pockets, he produced a pencil stub and a piece of paper. "This is his home number. He should be there now." Thrusting the scrap into her hand, Ray glanced over Leigh's shoulder to the room where the doctor was examining Missy. "I'll be right here."

Leigh nodded, her silvery hair glinting beneath the bright lights of the corridor. Long denim-clad legs carried her swiftly to the phone booth in the waiting area. The phone rang only once before it was answered.

"Dancer."

One word, honey-smooth; the liquid southern cadence held the authority of command and demanded respect of the listener. Despite the crisis, Leigh couldn't help appreciating the masculine tones.

"Mr. Dancer, you don't know me but Ray asked me to call you," Leigh began awkwardly, wishing she hadn't been so quick to offer her services as the bearer of bad news. She hadn't thought about how difficult it would be to call a complete stranger. For all she knew, he might well hang up on her without ever giving her a chance to explain.

"Ray who? My brother-in-law?" Joshua Dancer demanded, the blankness of the first question totally replaced by the concern in the second. "Is something wrong? Is it Missy? Has something happened?"

Leigh leaned her head against the wall, feeling helpless. "There has been an accident—" she began.

Joshua interrupted quickly. "Where? Tell me where they are and I'll be there."

Leigh supplied the name of the town and a concise explanation of the situation. She could not have been more surprised by his attitude. No questions, no useless demands to speak to Ray. Simply freely offered support and a promise to come. Once again Leigh wished she had been so lucky in her family and husband as Missy seemed to be. There would be no long lonely hours for this woman, locked in a struggle to save her child. Whether Missy lost her baby or not, she would know she was loved and wanted, not just by a husband but by a brother as well.

As Leigh walked back to join Ray she wondered what Joshua Dancer looked like. If his voice was anything to go by, he'd be sleek, with that cultured elegance of the old-style southern aristocrat. He'd be close to forty. The depth and mellow richness of his tone was no product of an untried male. He'd be—

Her mind came to a screeching halt as she realized what she was doing. Men, taken singly or as a whole, had no place in her life now, even one as admirable as Joshua Dancer seemed to be. She had no need to be speculating on his appearance. He could be fat, bald and ancient for all she cared.

But he wasn't, as Leigh discovered about an hour later. She'd been sitting in a hard chair, trying to pretend her nerves weren't feeling like shredded wheat. How she hated hospitals! Nothing she'd tried had made her feel any better about them since her own stay in one after the accident. Telling herself that it was weak and stupid to get all worked up about a building hadn't made a bit of difference. Already she was gritting her teeth, wishing she had never agreed to wait.

Leigh had no idea what made her glance up in time to see the tall, sable-haired man approach the nurses' station. He wore a sports coat and slacks that fit his body with custom-tailored perfection. He seemed completely relaxed, his arms loose at his sides, his hands quiet. He turned smoothly, with an economy of motion that was as effortless as it was effective. Leigh watched him stride toward her, mesmerized by the fluidity of his movements. Unaware that she was staring, she lifted her eyes to his face. Brows over eyes as black as the ace of spades created an expression that the old riverboat gamblers must have worn—rakish, decidedly male and not a little dangerous. Joshua Dancer was a man who knew who he was and in his knowledge gained command over more faint-hearted mortals.

Without conscious thought, Leigh rose from her chair. A weak position before this man was unthinkable. "Mr. Dancer, I'm the one who called you," she greeted, extending her hand. "I'm Leigh Mason."

Joshua took her hand and unconsciously held on to it while he scanned the slightly crowded room. "Where's Ray?" He glanced back at Leigh, too worried to be polite. When he knew how Missy was, then he would be able to exchange pleasantries. At another time he could have admired her serenity, the calm she seemed to radiate in the midst of the crisis. "Has there been any word?"

"She's still with the doctor. And there hasn't been any word, I'm afraid." She gestured to the chair beside hers. "We can see the door of the examining room Missy's in if we sit here."

Joshua glanced at the seat, then at the door across the hall. Waiting had never been his strongest virtue, especially when it came to someone he loved. "I think I'll see if I can't get some information. Surely they know something now."

"Missy must still be hanging in there," Leigh tried to reassure him. Now she could see the worry in his eyes. The relaxed stance had fooled her for a moment. "Missy hasn't lost the baby...." Her voice trailed away as she wished she hadn't put it that way. It sounded too stark, too emotionless.

Joshua inclined his head, seeing her regret but making no comment on it. "Then I guess we wait," he decided finally, his ebony gaze holding Leigh's.

Before Leigh could say anything else, a nurse joined them.

"Mr. Dancer, the doctor asked me to take you in to your sister now. So far everything is all right," she added, reading the need for reassurance in their expressions.

"I won't be long," Joshua said before turning to follow the woman across the hall.

Leigh stared after him, unable to believe she hadn't objected to his automatic assumption that she would be calmly awaiting his return. Eager to be gone and feeling unneeded now that Joshua Dancer was with his family, Leigh picked up her leather handbag and left.

She had done all that she could. It was past the time she usually went home. The atmosphere of the hospital was overwhelming her, and she could not stand it another minute. While she was needed she could push back the fear, the feeling of doom hospitals always brought to her. When the need was gone, so was her ability to control her desire to be free of its sterile walls.

Dutch whined his welcome as she slipped eagerly into the truck. "Time to be on our way, friend. We've done our good deed. Joshua's there, and that man's capable of handling anything. We're not needed here now." She had the pickup started and in gear before she finished speaking. A sharp turn and she was away, fleeing the memories that tried to pursue her. Instead she made herself think of the present and the life she had built for herself.

Business was booming. The renovation of her house on Dogwood was finally complete, and she had enough money in the bank to consider expanding her country-store operation to two locations. Yes, she was alone with no one and nothing depending on her except a few friends and her store. But it was the choice she had made when she cut all but one tie with her old hometown.

Leigh pulled into her driveway, shut off the engine and sat looking at the silhouette of one of her accomplished goals. She and Buddy had never had a real home, not one with tradition and heritage. Theirs had been a modern marriage with a sleek, gadget-filled apartment, young up-and-coming friends, planned births and money saved for vacations to the right places. She'd enjoyed that life, partly because she had never known any other, but mostly because she loved Buddy. But when the fabric of her existence had been torn apart by fate, when Buddy had stood at the end of her hospital bed and said he couldn't live with half a woman, she had hit bottom. Death would have been kinder, but the doctors had made sure she lived. To this day she wasn't certain whether to be glad or sorry their skill had saved her.

Her solitary existence had begun at that moment. She had left the hospital alone. A week later she had also left Chicago alone. She had driven until she was too tired to go any farther. Knoxville was where she had stopped and where she had put down roots. She hadn't been back to Chicago since, not to visit Jean or anyone else. Somewhere in the months that followed she had discovered that she needed tradition, a sense of belonging to something. The old house on Dogwood had satisfied part of her needs and her brainchild, Leigh's Country Crafts, the rest.

Dutch whined softly to be released, making her aware how long she had been sitting in the truck. "Sorry, guy," she apologized with a sigh. "I was woolgathering."

With a flick of her wrist she restarted the pickup and guided it into the garage. Turning the keeshond loose, Leigh entered the house through the connecting breezeway. The main building was white, with a wide veranda encircling its perimeter. Graceful columns across the front provided an elegant entrance that continued into the foyer with its crystal chandelier. Hooked rugs made by a woman in Pigeon Forge decorated hard oak floors, while crocheted bedspreads and canopies added a touch of old-world charm to the two bedrooms upstairs. Leigh had restored every corner, utilizing her skills as much as possible and only hiring out work when it exceeded her abilities. The result was all that she'd hoped for and more.

Realizing she was hungry, Leigh put the kettle on boil and placed a small quiche in the oven. Her footsteps echoed softly as she left the kitchen and entered the den to flip on the stereo. A moment later quiet music filled the house, courtesy of the hidden speakers she'd installed. After slipping off her boots, she returned to the kitchen where Dutch was waiting at the back door to be let in. Dog food poured in a huge dish satisfied the keeshond's hunger, while a quick shower and the comfort of a loose-flowing white caftan revitalized Leigh. A glass of chilled, pale wine was a perfect way to relax while she set the table for one.

The mushroom-and-broccoli entrée was light yet filling, the fresh strawberries and whipped farm cream a delightful ending for the meal. Leaving the dishes where they stood she retired to the den, her favorite room in the house. Dutch stretched out before the fireplace, while she curled into the soft cushions of the overstuffed sofa. Almost immediately her mind was assailed by past images she had consciously hidden away. Shying from the nightmare she couldn't change, she focused instead on the man who had cared enough to come the instant he was needed. Joshua Dancer wasn't a man a woman could easily forget or ignore. He had the kind of presence that would always make itself felt.

Yet what business did she have even thinking about him in view of her chosen life-style? It was unlikely she would see him again, anyway. Joshua Dancer. The name was familiar.

"I wonder where I've heard of him before," she mused out loud. The name just wouldn't leave her alone. She frowned as a memory pricked her consciousness.

"I've got it," she muttered, leaning over the arm of the couch to root in the magazine rack beside the sofa. Periodicals slithered in all directions as she shifted the pile with quick fingers. A moment later she pushed herself upright, slightly red in the face but triumphant, a magazine clutched in one hand.

"'Dancer investments—proven oracle for the moneyed elite,'" Leigh read aloud. "That picture sure doesn't do him justice."

The full-page color spread showed him dressed in a tux with a well-known, blond country-and-western star on his arm. To her eyes this one-dimensional Joshua conveyed only a fraction of the presence of the real man. Curiously, Leigh scanned the article. He'd started the business on a shoestring right out of college while working for moderately successful entertainers and small business people. A whiz with speculative deals. The instincts of a cardsharp.

"Not to mention the looks of a riverboat gambler," she mumbled, continuing her research.

One stepsister. Parents deceased. Unmarried and likely to remain so despite the woman in his life. Home office in Nashville. Branches in Atlanta and Knoxville.

"Wow!" she breathed, leaning back and letting the magazine slide unheeded to the floor. "No wonder he looked like he was king of this little corner of the world. He very well might be." She stared at Dutch, smiling slightly as his ears flickered back and forth at the sound of her voice. "You don't care, do you? You never liked men anyway."

The dog rose and padded to her; his dark eyes rimmed with the spectaclelike markings of his breed held silent intelligence. One buff-colored paw lifted to settle on her knee. His black-and-silver long-haired body was reassuringly solid, offering quiet comfort if not vocal agreement.

"I know. You're here." Leigh scratched gently behind his pointed ears. "It's too bad you can't talk as well."

With a sigh she got to her feet. It was late and although tomorrow was Saturday, it was still a workday. Switching off the den lights, she entered the hall. A sharp rap at the door caught her unawares. Startled, she jumped when Dutch barked. Grabbing his choke collar in one hand, she headed toward the entrance wondering who would be visiting at this time of night. It was well past ten.

"Who is it?" she demanded without opening the door.

"Joshua Dancer."

Leigh's eyes widened in shock. How had he found her? What did he want? Her hand hovered over the lock.

"Leigh, let me in."

"Why?"

"Because carrying on a conversation through a door is stupid."

She thought that one over. He was right. Why was she hesitating? Turning the bolt before she could change her mind, she found Joshua propped against the doorjamb with his hands in his pockets.

"You didn't wait."

"I'd done all I could. I'm a stranger to all of you. I would only have been in the way," she said, stating the truth as she saw it.

He looked tired. Harsh lines scored his brow and added deep creases at the corners of his mouth. His hair was ruffled as though he'd raked his fingers through the thick strands in frustration, helplessness or both.

"There's every reason," he corrected finally. "I owe you those kids' lives. And I always pay my debts."

Leigh leaned against the opposite jamb, her hand clenched around Dutch's collar. "Pay me?" she asked cynically, wondering if she could have misread the man. Perhaps he wasn't as caring as she had first thought. Only an insensitive person would offer money for her help. The flash of anger in his eyes was her only warning that she had hit a nerve.

Joshua straightened. "I've had a long night. My sister's just about to lose her baby and I'm hunting down the woman who risked her life on a deserted mountain road. When I said I owe you, I damn well didn't mean in dollars, although that could be arranged," he added, employing some sarcasm of his own. He continued before she could interrupt. "I meant I'm in your debt, and if I can ever serve you the way you did my family, then I want you to know I'll be there."

Their eyes met, each measured the other. Strangers—the gambler and the lady. Her strength had the supple lines of a willow; she had the unwavering gaze of one who believes in truth whatever the cost. His power was in the tough body no amount of tailoring could conceal and in the shrewd stare that assessed risks that made other men quail.

"I jump to conclusions sometimes," Leigh responded, meeting him halfway. There was something about Joshua that demanded an explanation rather than an apology.

"And I'm too blunt for polite society on occasion."

Her lips quivered at his resigned sigh. His matching grin showed off slightly crooked teeth. The little imperfection was reassuringly human.

"Why don't you come in?" she asked, smiling.

"I would if I'd been invited. Blunt I might be, but discourteous I'm not. Besides—" He paused to glance at the rigid keeshond at her side. "I don't relish being bitten by a wolf."

Laughing softly, Leigh eyed Joshua challengingly. "He's harmless as long as he's sure of your intentions."

Joshua stepped by her as she backed up. "They're strictly on the up-and-up," he promised, a dare gleaming in his eyes. "I never attack a beautiful woman before midnight."

Two

—

Startled at his teasing comment, Leigh stared at him. "I never said you did," she pointed out.

"Perhaps not, but I got the feeling that you thought it." Joshua's hard mouth quirked upward in challenge.

Leigh watched him steadily, intrigued despite herself. Some part of her mind registered the strange exhilaration of sparring with this man. "Are you always so blunt?" she asked finally, tilting her head to one side.

"When I have to be." Joshua shrugged, his gaze sweeping her from head to toe before settling on her face once more. "You look nothing like a woman who'd pull a daredevil stunt like stopping a runaway camper.''

Leigh barely kept a grin from breaking through at his remark. She'd never known anyone who hopped from one subject to another without a hint of direction. "Well, I did," she clarified, starting for the kitchen. She left it up to him whether to follow. If he could behave as though they knew each other well, then so could she.

"How old are you?" Joshua asked bluntly as he peered around the sunshine-yellow-and-pumpkin kitchen with interest. "Is there a Mr. Mason?"

Leigh paused in the act of filling the teakettle to glance over her shoulder. "Twenty-nine—and probably lots of them." She was more amused than irritated by his curiosity.

He frowned, his eyes flashing with summer lightning. "People who know me well would tell you that it's—"

"Not wise to bait the tiger," Leigh supplied cheerfully, unaffected by the mock threat. "I wonder why I'm not worried?"

Joshua moved closer. "Possibly because you've got more courage than sense," he suggested absently, studying her. Did nothing rile this woman? he wondered. She looked at him as though he were simply a creature to study. There was no awareness of him as a man in the quiet depths of her eyes. Without conceit he knew that that was not the usual reaction for a woman to have to him. The absence intrigued him, while raising questions as to why it should be this way.

Leigh swung around, watching him as closely as he did her. There was no denying that she was curious. She saw no reason why she could not indulge her curiosity since they wouldn't meet again after this.

"Would you like some tea?" she asked abruptly, suddenly needing to withdraw from the game. She had caught the spark of interest in Joshua's eyes. It had not been her intention to pique his masculine awareness. Foolishly it had not occurred to her that she was capable of doing so. For an instant she damned the solitary life-style that had made her forget how easily the male could be stirred. She didn't want Joshua, or any other man to be curious about her. Relationships meant risk, and she no longer had the nerve to take that risk. She had lost too much, so she did not play.

A feather-light touch on her cheek caught her attention. Leigh blinked, the painful memories sliding back into the dark corners of her mind where they lived.

"Don't look like that," Joshua commanded deeply, stifling the urge to take her in his arms. For a moment Leigh had looked so alone that it had torn at his heart.

She searched his face, mentally recoiling from the knowledge she saw written there. Somehow he had glimpsed her vulnerability. She felt naked before him, and the idea angered as well as frightened her. She wouldn't allow herself to be vulnerable to anyone or anything ever again.

"Like what?" she asked, voicing a question she never would have spoken if she had been thinking clearly.

"Like you're looking into hell," he answered, stepping nearer.

It was too much to take from a friend, much less a stranger. "You have no right."

"I'm taking it."

"No." The protest was wasted. He moved closer, his expression softening with every step she retreated. Leigh wanted to scream at him to stop. "I won't let you do this."

Joshua ignored her words, concentrating on her troubled face. "Is it past, present or future?"

"Leave it. Please." At least she sounded calm, even if she didn't feel it.

He caught her shoulders. "Answer me and I will."

"We're strangers."

"Sometimes that is the best person to tell. Think of it as partial payment on my debt if that makes you feel any better."

His words poured over her in a soft murmur. Part of Leigh recognized the gentleness of his voice and the hands that held her. She wanted no part of either. She couldn't allow herself the luxury. But she also knew determination when she saw it.

Leigh stared at him, wondering why she was even hesitating. Why didn't she just refuse and have done with it. "I'll answer this one question, no more." The bargain appeared out of nowhere.

He nodded slightly, signaling his agreement.

"Past."

"Can it be fixed?"

"You promised." It was an accusation and a plea for mercy.

"This is the last one. Don't you see I need to know?" His fingers tightened on her shoulders as though he would physically pull the answer from her.

Suddenly the control Leigh held over her emotions snapped. The wound had never healed. There wasn't even scar tissue over it to protect her from his probing. "It can't be fixed, damn you. And your questions are cutting me to ribbons. Leave me alone. I saved your family for you. What more do you want?"

Joshua could feel the tension in her, the pain. He wanted to protect her, but if he tried she'd claw him with words. He didn't want that. Why, he didn't know. All he knew for certain was that this woman had more courage than he'd seen in anyone, male or female, in a long time. Getting to know her was becoming more important by the second. Against his better judgment he voiced the need he had to take her in his arms.

"Let me hold you."

"No." She couldn't take much more. Her hands came up to lever some distance between their bodies. She would not give into the vulnerability that the night always brought: the need for someone to love her, to care so much that it didn't matter she was no longer whole.

"Then hold me, Leigh. For as God is my witness, I need you tonight. Missy's all I have left of my family.

I've raised her since she was thirteen. I could lose her and the baby she wants so much. I'm afraid," he pleaded. Seeing her pain had reminded him of his own—and of the fear he could not shake.

His confession had to be a trick. Joshua Dancer wouldn't admit to weakness, not the man who had carved a miniempire out of the glitter of the entertainment world. Leigh no longer trusted herself, her judgment or anyone. She had learned, the hard way, how easily lies tripped from the tongue.

Her cynicism must have shown in her eyes for Joshua smiled sadly, shaking his head. "You don't believe me."

"I don't know you well enough to believe you." She sounded hard. She knew it. Better to appear callous than to break down in tears. Knowing what Missy was going through was tearing at her insides. The other woman's pain was bringing back memories she had buried. "Missy can conceive again if this child is taken."

His recoil at her blunt pronouncement accomplished what all her protests had not. For a long moment he stared at her as though he couldn't believe she would say something so cold-blooded. Leigh ignored the look of shock. All that mattered was that she was free. It was all she would allow to matter.

"Now will you leave?"

"Damn you. You don't mean that. A woman who risks her life for total strangers couldn't mean that."

Leigh almost weakened then, almost reached out to him. Clenching her hands into fists, she stifled the urge to comfort him.

Joshua glanced at the betraying gestures, seeing them for what they were. He didn't understand but realized from her defiant stance that she wasn't about to allow him to try. Suddenly he gave up. He was too tired and too worried to do either of them any good.

"All right. Have it your way. I'll go."

The harsh words sounded angry to Leigh, as did the steps that carried Joshua out of the kitchen and through the front door. Leigh stood rigid until she was sure he was gone, then her control slipped away as though it had never existed. Sinking down onto a chair, she put her head in her hands and wept the tears she had dammed up for years. Sometime later she trudged up to bed, too emotionally empty to do more than fall asleep deeply. No nightmares, no dreams disturbed her solitude.

Joshua entered his hotel room, tossed his overnight case on the bed and then threw himself into a chair. He was a fool, a blunt-spoken jackass with more mouth than sense. It hadn't taken five minutes after he had left Leigh's to realize what he had done. He told himself that the worry over Missy and the near escape from injury, even death, she and Ray had had was no excuse.

He and Leigh were strangers. He'd had no right to demand answers about her past, especially when he could see it was tearing her apart to give them. She had given him back his family and he had repaid her in pain. The thought sickened him. He had to apologize, but he wasn't sure she'd allow him the opportunity. He wasn't even certain that he deserved the chance, he decided in disgust. But he also knew he couldn't leave things as they were.

Leigh lay in bed, staring out the window. The sun was just peeking over the cloud-traced horizon. A new day. How often in those early days after the accident had she wished never to see another sunrise? Now she always made it a point to watch every one. Most people would call that a sign of hope but she knew better. It was survival, pure and simple. Her life had been rebuilt on the principle that she could handle anything for twenty-four hours.

Keeping her mind blank of the events of the night before was easy only because the habit was so well learned. To remember was to hurt; to forget offered peace. If there had been a chance she'd have to see Joshua again, she would have been forced to face what had happened between them. As it was, she could safely ignore him and his questions. She went downstairs and let Dutch out before returning to shower and dress. Breakfast was next on the agenda, both for herself and Dutch, but first tea. After putting the kettle on she went to the back door to let the dog in. Oddly, he wasn't there. Dutch was never late for a meal. More curious than worried, she started down the path. The sight of the rigid keeshond in front of the back gate was surprising. Finding Joshua standing on

the other side of the barrier was a shock she would
have gladly done without.

"What are you doing here?" For the first time in
years she regretted her way of dealing with problems.
She wasn't prepared for this.

"I came to apologize and hopefully share my
breakfast with you." Josh held up a large box. "I
stopped at the bakery on the way over. These are fresh
out of the oven."

Leigh stared at him, unable to believe he thought it
was that simple.

"Please, Leigh. I regret last night more than I can
say. You were correct when you said I had no right to
pry into your life. Couldn't we start over?"

"There's nothing to start over." She wouldn't move
any closer. He was too near already.

"Don't you want to know how Missy is this morning?" The bribe wasn't much, but it was the best he
could do.

Startled, Leigh hesitated. Her first mistake.

Lowering the box, Joshua reached down and un-
latched the gate. He could feel Leigh watching him
warily, yet she made no protest. Not that she needed
to with the keeshond waiting with a distinctly hungry
look on his face.

"May I come in if I promise to behave?"

Leigh didn't move. She couldn't. "I don't really
think this is a good idea. We don't—"

Joshua interrupted before she could finish the refusal. "I'd offer a hostage to my good behavior if I

had one," he added, using every bit of charm he hoped he possessed.

Leigh studied him, wondering why she hadn't just turned around and gone back into the house. Dutch would have certainly come to heel if she had called him, or driven Joshua off if she had commanded it. Annoyed at her uncharacteristic indecision, she swore one short, pungent oath.

Hearing it, Joshua misunderstood. Was he hurting her again? An apology wasn't worth the price of her pain. Turning, he started to leave. He had taken two steps when she spoke.

"All right, but so help me, if you start with the questions again, I promise this time I'm going to sic Dutch on you even if I end up in jail."

Joshua barely controlled the pleased grin that he knew Leigh would misinterpret. Relief surged through him, surprising him with its power. He fully believed she was capable of doing just as she said, and oddly enough he admired her for it. He liked the strength and character hiding behind those pale eyes. Dependent women had never appealed to him.

Leigh called to Dutch, then turned to lead the way to the house. The teakettle was whistling when she entered with Joshua only a few steps behind her.

"Could we have a cup?" Joshua asked, watching her take the pot from the stove.

"If you like." Leigh didn't turn around as she answered. It was easier having him in her home when she wasn't looking at him. "Peppermint, apple-cinnamon or lemon?"

"Whatever you're having." While she made the beverages, Joshua opened the box of pastries. Immediately, the aroma of just-baked Danish filled the air. Dutch watched him suspiciously but with definite interest. Joshua eyed the dog, then decided to risk a finger with a bribe.

Leigh swung around just as he offered an icing-striped round to the keeshond. "He's trained not to take food from strangers."

Joshua glanced up, holding her gaze for a moment. "Then you give it to him," he said finally. He had heard the challenge, knowing it was a test about his intentions, but did Leigh also realize the significance of her words?

Leigh looked at Dutch to avoid Joshua's eyes. She'd been certain he would ask her to introduce him to her pet. The fact that he hadn't, disturbed her.

Joshua straightened to extend the treat to Leigh. "He's waiting."

Without taking the pastry from Josh, Leigh pointed at a spot in front of her. "Dutch, come." The dog sat waiting for her next command. Without looking at Joshua she placed her hand around his and gently offered it to Dutch to sniff. "Friend." The word was quiet but definite. Joshua's surprised indrawn breath was loud in the silence of the kitchen. "You can give it to him now. He'll eat it."

"Thank you."

The quiet words should have been unexpected. They weren't. Leigh lifted her head, compelled to face him. "I owe you an apology. Last night was rough on both of us. I forgot that." If she had been asked to explain why she had decided to trust Joshua even this much, Leigh knew she would've had no reply.

"You owe me nothing." Joshua could no more have stopped the hand he raised to her cheek than he could cease breathing.

For one moment Leigh allowed the light touch before she stepped back, putting a foot of space between them. "I'll make us some eggs to go with the Danish while you tell me about Missy."

Disappointed but determined not to show it, Joshua murmured, "I'd like that. I haven't had any breakfast, or any supper either now that I think of it." He would go slowly if it killed him.

So far so good, Leigh congratulated herself as she reached for the skillet. She was calm, in control, and Joshua wasn't crowding her the way he had last night. Maybe things weren't as intense as they had originally appeared.

"The silverware and the plates are in the hutch over there." After waving a long-handled fork vaguely in the direction of the far corner, she started separating bacon strips. Joshua was a big man, and he would need more than the scrambled eggs she'd planned for herself to keep him going. He had to be there if Missy needed him. The moment she realized where her thoughts had led her, Leigh stilled. This she could not allow. It was too easy to forget that Josh was just passing through her life. What was it about the man that made her feel as if she could sit down and talk to him one minute and wish she had never laid eyes on him the next?

"So how is she, this morning?" she asked when he made no attempt to break the silence between them.

"Holding her own. The doctor had already been by to check her when I called. As you can imagine, Ray is delighted."

"I'm glad."

Joshua paused to glance at her. The sincerity in her words was unmistakable, as was the suddenly rigid set of her shoulders. His hands clenched against the questions he'd promised he wouldn't ask. Every time he mentioned Missy and her child, Leigh was hurt. He could see and he could feel it. Had she had a child that had died? Had she been pregnant and miscarried? Somehow it didn't seem that simple. Questions and Leigh. The two belonged together.

"What are we eating?" He had to redirect his thoughts before his control broke.

"Eggs and bacon." Leigh glanced over her shoulder, her eyes alight with an unconscious relief. He hadn't pried into her past again. Finally she could really relax. Last night truly had been the product of an emotional day for both of them.

Joshua realized that, in some way only she understood, Leigh had decided to accept him. He knew if he made a move to change the status between them she'd retreat into her shell. "You don't need to go to this much trouble for me."

"Afraid I can't cook?"

"I don't think you would offer to do anything if you weren't capable of doing a good job. So I think I can trust my stomach to your hands."

Despite her best efforts, Leigh felt the heat rise under her skin. There wasn't one reason why she should blush at his words but she did. There had been no innuendo in his compliment, nothing beyond the simple statement of fact, yet she felt as if he had touched her.

Joshua's eyes sparked with fire at her reaction. "I had no idea women did that anymore," he observed, watching her closely.

"That depends on the woman." She didn't pretend to misunderstand.

"Have I embarrassed you?"

"Would it matter if you had?"

He thought a minute. "Yes, today it would. I'm on my best behavior, remember?"

Leigh had no reply and, fortunately, the bacon started popping to demand her attention. "How many eggs would you like?"

"Three if you don't mind."

Determined to keep the conversation on a more impersonal level, Leigh said, "Tell me about your work."

Joshua shot her a perceptive look, a gently mocking smile twisting his lips. "What do you want to know?"

"Everything, anything." Leigh handed him the platter of crisp bacon, and then began breaking eggs into a bowl.

Joshua came to stand beside her, his eyes following her movements. "Basically I advise people on how to use their money to the best advantage."

Ignoring his closeness and the silky cadence of his voice, Leigh concentrated on his words. "That sounds too simple to earn the description of being 'a wizard for the moneyed elite.'" A smile broke through at the pained look he gave her.

"That article is going to follow me to my grave," he muttered with a mild glare. "That crazy reporter would be better off writing fiction than doing interviews. He made me sound like some superhuman financial prophet. He's got half my clients believing Dancer Investments is infallible."

"Poor baby."

She had to laugh at his expression. It was a mixture of masculine disgust and mild outrage. He stood still at the sound. For a moment neither spoke. The tension was back, catching them unawares.

"Leigh, have dinner with me," Joshua said before he could think.

Leigh froze. "No, thank you," she refused politely, formally, mentally withdrawing.

"Why not? We both have to eat. I'll even promise to stay on my best behavior if that's what is worrying you."

"Please, Josh, don't push it. You are here because of your sister. As soon as she's well, you'll be going back to Nashville."

"So? Is there some law in Knoxville that says we can't have a friendly dinner together?" He *was* push-

ing, something he had never done in his life. But he
wanted her to go out with him more than any other
woman he had ever met. He had no explanation why
this was so, he just knew he couldn't let her refuse.

"I don't really have time," Leigh began, only to be
interrupted.

"Are you committed to someone?" It was the only
reason that made any sense.

"No." Leigh set the skillet of eggs aside before they
burned.

"Then why not? Tell me that and I won't say another word."

Leigh faced him, determined to put an end to his
interest once and for all. She had tried to be kind; now
she would be determined. "I've given you all the reasons I have. You'll just have to accept that I don't
want to go out with you."

Liar! The word lay in her mind like an accusation
but she ignored it. What she could not ignore were the
memories. It had been a long time since any man had
sparked her emotions the way this one did, and the
plain truth was that she was afraid to be alone with
him. She feared he would remind her of all she had
lost and all that she could never hope to have again.

Joshua saw and hated the shadows that crossed her
face. Leigh looked as vulnerable as the first flower of
spring. She'd made it clear, however, that he couldn't
help her.

"Can't we be friends?"

"What good would that do?" Leigh gave him a
straight look.

"How do I know?"

He raked his fingers through his hair. No matter what he offered Leigh was determined not to allow even a corner of her life to be touched by him. Even now he could feel her slipping away. He wanted to reach out and grab her, hold her, make her accept him by sheer force if necessary. The primitive urge shocked him for it had never been his way to pry and push into the lives of others. He was not a scalp collector hot on the trail of every female, either willing or unwilling, despite what the papers reported. Yet he couldn't let her go. Something inside him demanded he try to reach her despite the circumstances.

"We'd better eat before the eggs get cold." Leigh turned away, ending the conversation. One meal she could handle. More was asking for trouble and she'd had enough to last a lifetime.

Three

Leigh watched Joshua's car leave through a mist of gray drizzle. If she had been paying attention when she'd awakened, she would have known the weather was turning bad instead of being surprised by it when she opened the front door. As usual, Dutch had sped out into the rain, leaving her alone with Joshua. He had smiled, bid her goodbye, and even refused the raincoat she had offered to lend him. Leigh was thrown more off balance than ever by his behavior. He was acting like a casual friend and nothing more. That should have pleased her but it didn't. Frowning, she shut the door with unnecessary force, forgetting Dutch completely. She heard a loud bark before she had gone more than three steps, reminding her that the kees-hond was still outside.

"Fool dog," she muttered irritably, although Dutch's quirks would normally have had her smiling.

Her mood didn't improve with the cup of tea she carried upstairs before she dressed for work. Joshua's strange behavior bothered her, demanding attention that she didn't want to give. Telling herself that he was a temporary acquaintance brought into her life by unusual circumstances wasn't working. Neither was reminding herself that he had his life and she had hers. At some point during her musings she glanced at the bedside clock. She was going to be late if she didn't hurry.

Despite changing in record time, Leigh still managed to leave the house, Dutch at her heels, looking as she always did—sleek, feminine and definitely country. Slim-fitting, much-washed jeans embraced long legs to end in hand-tooled leather boots. A tailored blouse in pink-and-green plaid was open at the neck, giving a tantalizing glimpse of the shadowed valley between her breasts. Silver-white hair tumbled down to brush her shoulders, restrained only by two rose quartz hair clips. A slate-toned poncho kept off the rain when she made the dash from the truck to the store.

The rain was coming down with increased force when she pulled in behind Leigh's Country Crafts. The delivery entrance was only a few steps away, but that wouldn't help much with all the merchandise waiting to be unloaded in the back of the truck.

"Hi, boss," Leigh's assistant, Sally, greeted her cheerfully as she entered the store. "Gorgeous day out, isn't it?"

Leigh grimaced, wiping the raindrops from her cheeks with her fingertips. "If I were a duck it would be," she agreed dryly. "I don't think I've ever met anyone who gets as turned on by wet weather as you do." Leigh studied the bouncy brunette curiously. "What is it with you and rain?"

Sally shrugged slightly plump shoulders, her brown eyes twinkling mischievously. "Will and I got married in the rain. In fact, it stormed our whole honeymoon." Her grin was alive with hot-blooded memories.

Leigh laughed, unable to resist Sally's uninhibited delight in just plain living. Her assistant was five years older than her, looked and acted ten years younger and faced every day with an exuberance unmatched by anyone Leigh had ever known. Sometimes Leigh was sure Sally would embrace the world if she could just get her arms stretched wide enough to do it. It was that open, uncomplicated friendliness that made Sally such an asset to Country Crafts. No customer ever went away without feeling as though he or she had made a friend. It was also that same trait that had made it impossible for Leigh not to be drawn into a deep and lasting friendship with Sally.

"So what are we doing today, as if I didn't know?" Sally asked, interrupting Leigh's thoughts.

"We're unloading the goodies," Leigh replied with a grin. "Just wait until you see the things I brought back this time. We really made out like bandits."

"Hot dog," Sally enthused. "Did Grandma Haynes have stuff for us, too?"

Leigh nodded, feeling the excitement of handling the mixed collection of treasures build. Her crafts people were more than practitioners of often long-forgotten skills. Their creations not only displayed the scope of their individual artistic talent but were also a piece of America's heritage.

"She sent the most exquisite crocheted bedspread I've ever seen. I don't know how I'm going to bring myself to part with it."

"Then don't," Sally returned promptly. "You've got three bedrooms, so you must have a bed to fit it."

Shaking her head at this impractical solution, Leigh stepped out into the rain for the first of many trips. Sally stood at the back door to take each carefully protected box. It was almost an hour later before Leigh closed the tailgate and returned to the shop. Sally was waiting with two hot cups of tea.

"One thing about days like this, it makes it easier to do stock. Most of our customers will stay home and dry." So far neither of them had been interrupted even once to wait on anyone since the shop opened.

"And that's a blessing?" Leigh queried, one brow arched.

Sally chuckled at her disbelieving expression. "It's a good thing I know you aren't the serious, ambitious person you pretend to be."

"Don't kid yourself. I am ambitious and serious," Leigh corrected, puzzled. "You know that."

Frothy brown curls bobbed once over a face wiped clean of amusement. "You are and you aren't. I think there's a romantic hiding inside that pragmatic store owner."

Leigh froze, rejecting the description with every nerve. Romantics were dreamers, sensitive, prey to the least slight and easily hurt. Maybe she had been one of those a lifetime ago but no more. She no longer believed in illusions and happily ever after. Fate had taught her to accept only what she could hold in her hands and never—not ever—care too much for even that.

"I'm not the romantic; you are," she declared in what she hoped was a normal tone. Lifting her mug, she finished the last sip of tea, which she no longer wanted.

Sally peered at her, started to say something, then changed her mind. "I can't wait to see what's in the boxes," she stated instead, glancing around the crowded storeroom-and-office combination.

Breathing a carefully concealed sigh of relief, Leigh followed her gaze. Spicy scents filled the air, courtesy of the spice ropes, lace sachet bags and pomanders lining one shelf. Stuffed calico cats shared places with rag dolls, corn-husk miniatures and wood carvings. The bits of almost-forgotten crafts testified to the diversity of the store's stock, while the gaping, empty spaces warned of dwindling supplies.

"Let's get to it," Leigh decided, lifting the first carton onto the worktable for unpacking.

Sally took up the handwritten inventory, checking off each item as Leigh unwrapped it. They worked in harmony, stopping only to attend to an occasional rain-dampened customer. It was well into the afternoon before the last of the new arrivals began finding their way to the store shelves. Leigh was in the home-linens section arranging a display of Grandma Haynes's crocheted masterpieces while Sally greeted yet another shopper. Leigh's fingers lingered over the delicate blue-and-cream lap robe she had just draped in soft folds against a lace-and-ribbon-trimmed pillow. The downy feel reminded her of the baby blanket—

"I like that."

The deep male voice startled her. Leigh swung around, catching her toes on the box at her feet. Off balance, she lurched into the hard body only a few inches from her own. Strong arms caught her close, steadying and supporting her while she regained her footing.

Leigh pulled away from his chest and raised her chin to stare at the cause of the ungainly greeting. Ebony eyes shone with silent amusement, and something else that she had no intention of acknowledging.

"Do you always sneak up on people like that?" she demanded, trying to subdue an urge to rest against him a little longer. Darn, he looked good. The rain had darkened his hair and left it falling in unruly waves over his forehead.

"I didn't sneak," Joshua murmured before swooping down to find her lips. They parted in surprise at his caress, affording him an entry she never would have granted otherwise. He took advantage of it, knowing the risk he was running, but not caring. He'd been aching to hold her, to kiss her, from almost the first moment he'd been in her home.

Shock—and the sudden unfamiliar quivering in her knees—kept Leigh unresisting in his embrace for long seconds. She felt his lips move with practiced finesse on hers, his tongue probing with a seductive thrust that invited a response. Her arms were beginning to slip up to his shoulders when sanity abruptly asserted itself.

Leigh wiggled suddenly, escaping his cradling hold and ducking under his arm to retreat the few steps the limited space allowed.

"That's cheating!" she gasped, annoyed at him and herself. How could she have responded?

Joshua came toward her, a smile on his lips. "No, it isn't." He spread his hands in apology. "Would you believe I forgot myself for a moment?"

"No," she denied swiftly, glaring at him. Every instinct warned her that if she believed that, she'd better be ready to buy the Brooklyn Bridge from the first con man who came down the pike.

Joshua shook his head, his eyes shielded briefly behind long lashes. "Somehow, I knew you'd say that," he replied sadly, a lurking grin belying his penitent tone.

Leigh debated forgetting her manners long enough to throw something at him after that mocking remark. The memory of where they were stopped her. Business owners *did not* toss merchandise at people, no matter what the provocation. Besides the only missiles handy wouldn't have hurt a butterfly.

Joshua crossed his arms over his chest, watching her battle her emotions. He knew he'd slipped under her defenses, but he couldn't make himself regret his tactics. This woman had extraordinary composure. It was only when he caught her off guard that he got a glimpse of the fire in her. The calm settling over her features drew a disappointed sigh.

"I really came by to pick up some gifts for Missy," he explained before she could speak. The wariness and skepticism in her eyes bothered him, even while he admitted silently that he deserved part of the latter.

"What kind of presents?" she asked after a short pause.

"I'm not sure. I was hoping you'd have some suggestions," he confessed, hardly paying any attention to his words. Instead he listened to her voice, marveling at the slow, smoky rhythm of her speech. He found her voice infinitely pleasing to his ears. The frown, however, now lining her brow, he could do without.

"I'd need to know more about Missy's likes and dislikes," she informed him finally, wondering what game he was playing. "Do you want something personal, cheerful, sweet or what?"

Faced with that many choices, Joshua felt like giving up before he started. Why hadn't he remembered the horror of shopping for Christmas and birthday presents?

"I want to give Missy something pleasant and maybe even fun to think about for the next few days. The doctor has said she's to stay in the hospital until Monday. I thought a present a day might help the time go faster."

Leigh stared at him, touched in spite of herself at the caring and sensitivity his idea showed. She couldn't help but remember her own long days in the hospital, and know that what he had in mind would have lightened the dark hours.

"What about a little of each?" she suggested, turning to lead the way to the ladies-wear section. Stopping before a counter displaying cobweb-fine lace sweaters, scarves and bed jackets, Leigh lifted a delicate mohair creation. The almost weightless froth of buttercup-yellow was as soft as thistledown in her hands.

"How about this for a start? Hospitals can make a woman feel so unfeminine. Something frilly might be just the ticket." She held out the fragile garment. Slender, sunshine-bright ribbons fluttered gently with the movement.

Joshua looked at Leigh, then at the jacket she held. For the first time he really saw the store and its crafts as something more than Leigh's business. The intricate workmanship, obvious to even his untutored eyes, raised the goods that she sold to far above the ordinary.

"It's perfect. How could it not be?" he replied truthfully, reaching out to stroke the fine wool lightly. "Missy wears a lot of yellow, too." He glanced up in time to catch Leigh's pleased smile. His breath lodged momentarily in his throat at the beauty of the simple gesture. It was as gentle and as startling as a rainbow after a summer shower.

"You're beautiful."

Leigh met his gaze, unable to look away from his unblinking study. The deep, husky voice sank slowly into her mind, warming and exciting her at the same time. His expression was serious, revealing a quiet intensity she was becoming familiar with. She could see Joshua meant the compliment. It had been a long time since she had considered herself more than a flawed creature, an empty shell that once a man, her husband, had thrown away. Beautiful! One word, yet so painful.

For a split second, a surge of unfamiliar emotion blocked her speech. Then the unreality of the situation came to her rescue once more. The Leigh she had built so painstakingly from the ashes of the past, the slightly cynical, no longer naive and trusting creature, came rapidly to the fore.

"Not really. I'm too pale," she informed him calmly.

"And moonlight across the snow is pale, too," he returned softly, wondering what memory his words had drawn from the darkness of her past. He resisted the urge to touch her by reminding them both of the gifts for Missy they had yet to find.

Momentarily confused, Leigh was slow to respond. The gentle look in his eyes as he waited for her to adjust to the change worried her as much as the sexual tension he could weave about her, seemingly at will.

"How about a pretty lace pillow filled with scent?" Holding the bed jacket much too tightly, Leigh gestured toward the shelf of sachets a few feet away. "You look while I give this to Sally to wrap."

Barely waiting for his agreement, Leigh hurried off. She needed both time and space. Only one was possible. Like a coward, she took what she could get. In the end her tactics gained her little more than a momentary respite. It took more than an hour for Joshua to decide on the other presents for Missy. What had started out as a search for three gifts had ended up as a stack of a half-dozen packages, wrapped in Leigh's Country Crafts blue-and-cream floral paper. Fluffy bows of ribbon and lace decked the lot.

"I'll take these three with me for giving when I visit. The rest I'd like delivered."

Leigh was so concentrated on the technicalities of the delivery that she almost jumped when Joshua glanced at her and said, "I'd like to take you out to dinner tonight. A kind of thank-you, if you like, for all your help today. Will you come?"

Leigh felt like hitting him. He knew darn well she didn't want to have dinner with him tonight or any other night. It didn't help her mood to see Sally grinning while she tried to find a polite way to refuse.

"I don't think she likes me." Joshua slanted a smile at Sally, who laughed softly.

"She has a temper," she warned.

"I know."

Leigh glared at them both. "I don't think either of you is funny." It was a good thing there was no one else in the store. She should have known she was wasting her breath. Sally had been trying for the past year to get her interested in men, any man. Joshua was just the type to get her romantic friend in a match-making mood again.

Joshua held up his hands in surrender. "I know when I'm not wanted. I'm going."

Before Leigh could agree, he was gone, leaving the tiny bells that hung above the front door weeping softly.

"That is one sexy male," Sally murmured finally.

Leigh inclined her head. A vocal agreement was beyond her at the moment.

"Nice too."

Another nod.

"I like him."

This one was easier. "You like everyone."

"He likes you."

"Perhaps. I'm going to get back to work. Call me if you need me."

Leigh may have thought she'd finish restocking, but the best-laid plans rarely, if ever, turn out as anticipated. The rain stopped five minutes after Joshua left and as the sun came out so did the customers. Leigh and Sally were so busy they barely had time to draw a breath.

The store was late in closing, and by then the rain had returned with greater force than before. The change in the weather did nothing to improve Leigh's mood. All afternoon she'd been strangely unsettled, almost as if she was waiting for something to happen. It did. Her tire was as flat as a pancake and she hated changing it in a drenching downpour. She was turning back to retrace her steps when she saw Joshua. His car was parked a space away, easily visible if she hadn't been concentrating on keeping her footing on the wet ground.

Joshua rolled down his window. "Come on. Get in and I'll take you home."

Leigh hesitated. Rain was leaking around the hood of her raincoat, soaking the clothes underneath. She couldn't seem to either walk away or go toward him.

"What are you doing here?"

"Waiting for you."

Three words, spoken in the most unlikely of settings. Yet she believed him. Was this what she'd been waiting for all afternoon?

"Get in, Leigh."

"I'm not going out with you." One step closer.

"I know. I'm just offering my car as a taxi."

"You'll drop me off, then leave." Two more steps nearer.

"If you like."

"My truck."

"Lock it. You can call the repair people from your house."

"You could change it," she said.

"So could you," he countered.

"It's wet out here."

He laughed at that and, after a moment, so did she. "Then why don't you come in from the rain? Are you afraid?" He couldn't resist the goad and was surprised when it worked. Leigh slipped into the car bringing the wet with her.

"I'm not afraid of anyone." She glared at him as though daring him to disagree.

"You might not be, but I am," he murmured beneath his breath before starting the car.

Four

———

"You're very quiet."

Leigh glanced away from the rain-drenched windshield to Joshua's face. The streetlights cast an intermittent glow in the car, highlighting the angles and deepening the shadows of his features. There was strength in him, gentled now.

"I shouldn't have let you take me home." The words escaped without thought. "It's out of your way."

How much should he tell her? A quick look warned him that Leigh was gathering her defenses again. Josh stifled a sigh of frustration. Leigh was more difficult to handle than his most temperamental client. One wrong word and she was away. Cynical, distrustful, wary, beautiful, hurt and vulnerable described her, yet didn't begin to capture the essence of the creature who looked as if a strong wind would blow her away. The stillness she could effect the moment he breached her defenses told more than her words. Thank God her distrust of him seemed based on her past rather than anything he had said or done. That fact and her courage gave him hope.

He had decided to bide his time, concentrating on maneuvering his way into her life in the most non-threatening way possible. He was too wise a man to ask her point-blank questions after the few he had ventured had met with such a total lack of success. Instead he planned a subtle campaign. This morning had been the first step.

"I was waiting for you. I came straight from the hospital. I wanted to tell you how much Missy enjoyed the bed jacket."

"How is she?" Leigh couldn't stop the question. Twice, she had almost picked up the phone to check on the younger woman, and then changed her mind at the last minute.

"No change but according to her doctor that's a good sign."

"I'm glad."

Joshua turned the car into Leigh's drive and shut off the engine. "Could I talk you out of a cup of coffee?"

Leigh started to refuse, then hesitated. He had brought her home. It didn't seem fair to send him away on a night like this.

"All right. One cup of coffee."

Neither his pleased smile nor the hamper he collected from the back seat was reassuring. She had no time to demand an explanation before they got out of the car. No one but an idiot stood in the pouring rain and argued. Dutch jumped out behind them with a low bark of joy at the muddy conditions of his territory. The back door might have been only a few feet away and partially protected by the breezeway, but it made little difference. The rain was coming down harder by the second and the wind had begun to kick up. She and Joshua entered the kitchen at a trot, just managing to slam the door against a strong gust of wind.

Leigh peeled off her raincoat and hung it on the rack beside the door. Turning, she found Joshua had done the same. The hamper sat on the floor at his feet.

"What's that?"

He glanced down then back at her. "Dinner."

She was shaking her head before he had finished the word. "I didn't agree to that."

"I cheated."

"You're always cheating."

"Only on good things."

"By whose opinion?"

"Mine and, I hope, yours." He bent over, lifted the basket and placed it on the counter. "I saw that mass of stock you were working on. I know you took over an hour helping me find Missy's presents. I thought you might be tired after a day like that and would probably not feel like cooking when you got home. I took a chance you'd share this with me."

Joshua waited. He'd never given such a long excuse for an impulse in his life. It was a good thing he wouldn't need to tell her what else he had done.

Leigh realized that once again Joshua had her. To refuse would be senseless and overreactive. It was only a meal after all—and a very thoughtful gesture as well. So why was she feeling stalked? There wasn't anything in his voice or his actions that should make her uneasy, but she was. Watching him closely, she said, "All right. We'll eat together."

"I don't know about you but I'm damp and a little chilled. Would you mind if I lit a fire? We could eat in front of it as well."

Warning bells went off in Leigh's head. He had to be up to something—the basket, the picnic-style food in front of a fire, a rainy night. It all added up to seduction. Forewarned was forearmed, she reminded herself as she agreed to his suggestion.

But it didn't work out that way. It was one thing to prepare yourself for an attack and win. Quite another to be alert and ready for a confrontation that never materialized. Joshua did just what he said: he lit a fire, laid out the food and ate. True, they talked but certainly not along the lines Leigh had been prepared for. Instead they spoke of the one thing she would have preferred forgotten. The rescue.

"After I left you this morning, I rode out that road where you helped Missy and Ray."

Startled, Leigh glanced up from the slice of cheese-cake she had just served herself. "Why?"

"Curiosity." He swallowed once, remembering the sheer drop-off that had almost been Missy's last vision of earth. If it hadn't been for Leigh and her daring, there would have been no tomorrows for his sister.

Leigh saw the anguish in his eyes. She was intimately acquainted with that kind of pain. Without thought, she reached out to a man who she didn't understand or even fully trust.

"It didn't happen," she said quietly.

Ever since he had seen the scene of the accident, Josh could not believe anyone would have knowingly put themselves in the kind of danger that Leigh had. Only a person who had no thought for the future would take a risk like that. Yet Leigh did not seem to be that type of woman. Her home and her business indicated a need of stability, of security.

"It could have," he grated harshly. "You could have been killed as well. Did you think of that?"

The answer emerged, more telling than Leigh would have allowed if she had been thinking clearly. "It didn't matter."

Shocked, Joshua stared at her. She meant it!... The idea was inconceivable.

His hand tightened on hers while his eyes probed her expressionless face. "Why, Leigh? Why would a woman like you say such a thing? Much less believe it? And God knows you do for I can see it in your eyes."

Leigh tried to escape but he held her securely, thwarting her bid for freedom.

"Let me go."

"I can't. I need to know. I know you don't think I have the right. I even agree, but it's important to me to understand. That was my sister out there. She would be maimed or dead but for you. Why did you do it?"

Leigh said nothing, only waited for her freedom and the end of questions that pierced her like sharp knives. She could not make herself trust him. She did not dare.

Joshua knew the strength of her silent refusal was equal to his need to know. If only she trusted him. If only he dared push her just a bit more. Perhaps anger would accomplish what asking would not. For a split second he was tempted to goad her. He fought the impulse when he remembered the pain his last blundering probing had caused her. He couldn't risk hurting her even for the answers that were becoming so vital to him. Slowly, he released her hand.

"The rain is slackening off a bit. I guess I'd better go."

Leigh stared at him as he rose. He was leaving, just like that? Hadn't she won? Hadn't he finally backed off? She wanted to ask but was afraid to know. So she watched while he reloaded the picnic basket then silently headed for the kitchen. Scrambling to her feet, Leigh followed him. Josh was slipping on his raincoat when she reached him.

Joshua lifted his head to study her as she stood poised in the doorway. "Would you remember one thing for me?"

The oddity of his request barely impinged on Leigh's mind. It was the hesitant words that got her attention. "That depends," she allowed cautiously.

He smiled sadly. "I have no reason to hurt you and every reason to protect you. You gave me back my family. I won't forget that. If you need proof of your safety with me, remember that."

He permitted her no time to answer. He was gone with only a swirl of rain-scented wind to mark his departure from her home.

A roll of thunder penetrated Leigh's sleep. Groaning, she pushed her head under the pillow and tried to shut out the noise. It was impossible. If anything the sound increased in volume. Finally she woke up enough to realize it wasn't thunder but someone knocking on her door. Normally she wasn't given to swearing, but after the night she'd had she felt justified in painting the atmosphere blue.

"Damn Joshua and his questions."

They had plagued her relentlessly, stealing her sleep until exhaustion had come to the rescue. Now some obnoxious person was interrupting the hours of lost sleep that she might have been able to make up. She flung open the front door to find the object of her thoughts on her porch, leaning against the jamb.

"Go away." She started to slam the door. His foot stopped her.

"Rough night? Let me make you some coffee."

"No."

"I brought breakfast." He held up a bag. "Hot cinnamon buns with lots of icing."

She glared at him. "I've heard that one before. This time I'm not buying."

Joshua ignored her words. He'd seen the fear in her eyes, fear that was so much a part of her that she probably no longer noticed its existence.

"I thought after breakfast we'd go by to see Missy. She wants to thank you for the jacket in person."

Leigh wasn't budging an inch. This time his tactics weren't going to get him anything but a refusal. "You bought it, I didn't."

"You helped pick it out."

"She doesn't know that."

"Yes, she does. Besides she needs the company. And it's Sunday. You don't have to work."

"Maybe I have other plans...."

"Do you?" he returned swiftly, daring her to lie.

Leigh seriously considered it. In the end her integrity won the battle over her instinct for survival. "No."

"Missy's young and she's scared, although she's pretending not to be. Won't you take pity on her?"

"I hate the way you always make me feel like I'm either discourteous or selfish whenever I don't immediately fall in with your plans," she muttered, stepping back to allow him to enter.

Leigh wasn't really angry at him and that surprised her. If anyone else had arrived this way she would have been. He had forced her hand more than once, but still she let him get closer to her than anyone had in a long time. At some point in the wee hours of her sleepless night she had finally admitted the truth to herself even if she couldn't admit it to him. Her bravery—his words not hers—didn't extend to answering his questions but it did allow her to enjoy having him around. He might make her angry enough to throw things, but he also gave her moments of caring that had been absent in her life for so long. The idea was not one she welcomed, but she was honest enough to see it existed.

Joshua controlled an ill-advised grin; sending her into a temper was the last thing he wanted to do. "I'm sorry."

"No, you're not so don't say you are." Leigh returned dryly, gesturing toward the kitchen. "You know where everything is. I'm going to get dressed."

A few minutes later Leigh closed her bedroom door, her hands shaking as the realization of what she had just agreed to sank in. Except for two nights ago, she hadn't been inside a hospital since she had been discharged from the one in Chicago after the accident. Now she had not only committed herself to visiting one but to seeing a pregnant woman in the same type of setting where she had lost her own child. The idea made her sick to her stomach. It did no good to tell herself that her phobia was irrational. It hadn't worked the other night so why should it work now? No amount of reasoning had ever been able to erase the memory of the doctor beside her bed saying she had lost her baby, that he had cut out part of her body to save her life. Or the memory of Buddy, a few weeks later, telling her he wouldn't be there when she came home, that he couldn't live with what had happened to her and to their child.

"I can't," she moaned out loud.

The whimper of pain shocked her out of the immobility of her stance. She had to get control of herself. If Joshua saw her like this, with her defenses down, she'd never be able to put him off. Heaven help her, she wasn't even sure she'd have the strength to fight him if he did insist on an explanation. At that moment she wasn't sure which was worse, facing the hospital or having Joshua see her weaknesses. A second later Leigh had her answer. Going through life burdened by this irrational fear was not to be contemplated. Realizing that she did not want Josh to know about her phobia had shown her fear in a new light. For that if nothing else she was grateful to him.

Joshua had tea ready when she returned to the kitchen. Even the table was set, the cinnamon buns warm and fragrant on a platter in the center.

"This is getting to be a habit." The comment was more to break the silence than an attempt at real conversation. He was watching her much too closely for her peace of mind. Her control was paper thin as it was.

"A pleasant one, I hope." Joshua carried the teapot to the table.

She wouldn't answer that one if he paid her. "These look delicious." Sitting down quickly, she took one of the iced squares and placed it on her plate.

Joshua frowned, not liking the brittle way she spoke or the tense way she moved. Something was amiss and it wasn't the same thing that had been wrong when she opened the door to him earlier. He couldn't ask, so he guided the conversation into what he hoped was a relaxing direction.

"Missy was really impressed with the workmanship in her jacket. She asked me all kinds of questions so I hope you're prepared to have her do the same to you. She's into crafts. In fact she's just about drowned me in knitted socks and sweaters over the years."

Grateful for the diversion, Leigh didn't question how he had known that she needed one. She just accepted it. "It's amazing how the old arts that have almost died out are making a dramatic comeback. Sally and I get as many questions on where to go to get lessons as we do on the crafts themselves."

"Do you do any of the work you sell?"

"Not really. I don't have the time. Although I have made some things for the house."

"What got you interested in handicrafts? Your mother?"

Leigh laughed, her first completely natural reaction of the morning. "No way. My mother was the original career woman. If it couldn't be bought in a store or made from a packaged mix, she didn't want anything to do with it."

"Then how—"

Leigh didn't let him finish. "I used to be like her. One day I discovered it wasn't enough. I went hunting for tradition and old values. I found them here. I started Country Crafts because I needed a way to earn a living.''

The answers were too pat. Her gaze too direct, too filled with challenge. Joshua wanted to ask questions and knew he wouldn't get the first answer if he did.

''From the reaction of the nurses on Missy's floor I'd say you were very successful in your decision.''

Leigh released the tension that had held her still with a careful sigh. ''I've been lucky in the artisans that work for me.'' Leigh finished her cinnamon bun, knowing she couldn't put off their departure any longer.

Joshua downed the last swallow of coffee. ''Are you ready?''

Leigh rose, saying, ''Just let me get Dutch his ice cube.''

''I'll get the dishes,'' he offered, then asked, ''Why an ice cube?'' The idea of the large dog and an ice cube was startling and not easily understandable.

''He likes ice. He has since a puppy. So I use it as a combination bribe and reward when I leave him home.'' She shrugged lightly. ''He'd eat fifty of them a day if I'd let him.'' She finished locking the back door. ''We can go out the front.''

Joshua followed her down the hall and onto the porch. The sun poured gold over the bright flowers in the yard. There are so many facets to this woman, Joshua thought as he watched her close the door behind them: a dog who looked like a wolf and ate ice cubes like a child, the house filled with treasures of a bygone era, a yard alive with color and fragrance, and a business that drew numerous compliments. When she stood there with sunlight in her hair, a man could be forgiven for thinking her beauty was all there was to the woman. He knew better. A past that scraped with razorlike talons too often for his liking lurked in those eyes. She stood alone. He wondered if she ever cried out in the night for someone to hold her. If she did, he knew she would never admit it—any more than she would admit that something about Missy, the hospital or both scared her almost speechless.

The drive to the hospital was carried out in a steadily growing silence. Joshua tried to carry on a conversation but Leigh's monosyllabic answers were no help. She grew tenser with each mile. To him the change was dramatic. That bleak expression he was coming to hate was back on her face yet again. He wanted to demand she talk to him, to tell him what hurt her. But all he could do was sit there and drive. Whatever held her stiff and silent was not something she would share with him.

Finally, they arrived at the hospital. He parked the car, but he didn't think Leigh was more than marginally aware they had stopped. Her gaze was riveted to the building before them. He reached out to touch her arm, but she didn't show any sign she felt his hand. He could almost feel the pain in her.

"Leigh, let me take you back." The words slipped out without thought. Anything was better than the resigned silence that shouted acute suffering.

"No. I have to do this." Her voice was so quiet that he had to bend forward to hear her.

"Can you tell me why?"

Leigh looked at him then. "I wish I could," she whispered, meaning it. For the first time in a long while she didn't want to be alone. The faint words floated between them, delicate and fragile as a butterfly but with all the power of a bolt of lightning.

Joshua caught her hand in his, its weightless feel tugging at him in a way nothing else ever had. She was so fragile, so vulnerable. Every instinct in him demanded its freedom to protect her, to ease the pain he saw in her eyes, but he could do nothing. She denied him and herself. Frustrated, helpless, it was all he could do not to pull her into his arms and keep her there until she told him of the demons that threatened her.

"Let's go in before I lose my nerve." Leigh returned the hard pressure of his hand, grateful for the silent strength he offered. Most of all she was grateful for the questions he didn't ask. She couldn't have born those without breaking. Not now, not when she felt like a single touch would shatter her into a thousand pieces.

"I know I don't have the right to say this." Joshua watched her, hoping she wouldn't refuse him this time. "Let me help you. Call it a repayment of what I owe you if you must. But don't shut me out."

Leigh tried to pull her hand free, more hurt than she cared to admit at his reference to the debt he felt he owed her. She didn't want his help because of what she had done for Missy and Ray. Better nothing than that. Even as she thought it, she knew her attitude was contradictory and in a way a lie. Joshua was too strong a man to use such a flimsy excuse. He was giving her an out. The fact that he realized she might need one showed a greater knowledge of her personality than the short forty-eight hours of acquaintance allowed for.

"I'll remember." For one moment she indulged herself to cling to his strength. Then she released his hand swiftly. "Let's go. Missy's waiting."

Five

———

I'm so glad you could come."

Missy's soft voice washed over Leigh in gentle waves as she approached the bed on which the younger woman lay. Except for the obviously clinical nature of the surroundings, Missy looked the picture of health. Her silky brown hair lightly touched delicately flushed cheeks and her eyes were clear and warmly welcoming. Leigh felt some of the tension flow out of her as she realized the pain she had expected was not nearly as strong as she'd feared. Missy's case was far different than her own had been when she had lain in a hospital bed and watched the door for the visitors who rarely came. For a moment Leigh felt envious of Missy and the people who loved her. There was regret, too.

Her own life would have been different if she had had Buddy to depend on when she had needed him. She would have still been in Chicago building a career, for him and—

Her thoughts came to a screeching halt. No, she did not regret the past, she realized with a flash of insight. Without it she never would have let everything she knew help her to try to make another place for herself. She would never have found the fulfillment her business gave her. A small smile touched her lips, and she was able to move forward to return Missy's greeting, feeling freer than she had in a long while.

"How are you?" Leigh asked, suddenly conscious of Joshua's silent appraisal. He was close, less than a step away. She could feel his unquestioning support and marveled at its presence. No one, not even Buddy in the early days of their marriage, had ever offered her so generously of themselves. The effect was as unexpected as it was powerful.

Missy grinned, her dark brown eyes filled with unblemished happiness. "I'm going home tomorrow. Isn't that fantastic?"

"You're darn right it is, woman," Ray agreed, beaming at her from the chair beside the bed. "We really were lucky." He carried his wife's hand to his lips before turning to look at Leigh. "And we owe it all to you. If you hadn't—"

Leigh held up her palm, knowing what was coming. She didn't want thanks. "Don't, please. I was there and we were all lucky. I've never done anything like that in my life. I could have pitched us over the edge, you know."

"Leigh, why don't you have a seat?" Joshua inserted on seeing Leigh's discomfort at the praise.

"Yes, have my chair," Ray said. "I can sit on the bed."

Leigh glanced at Joshua under the cover of her lashes, grateful for his intervention. His slight smile said that he knew and understood her reluctance to discuss her part in the rescue. A second later the reality of their unspoken communication touched Leigh, creating a faint stir of uneasiness. Before she had a chance to do more than register the presence of the new sensation, Missy spoke, reminding her of where she was.

"Not if Mrs. Baumgarner comes in, he can't," Missy argued, looking quickly at the closed door as though expecting an invasion.

Glad of the diversion Missy's comment provided, Leigh sat down determined to remember why she was in the hospital room. "Don't tell me you have a white-coated drill sergeant," she remarked with a sympathetic grin.

Missy nodded, a grimace tightening her pink lips. "She's as strict as my third grade teacher," she confided engagingly.

"Then you must be giving her trouble, Sis," Joshua pointed out with a brother's unwelcome candor. Casually perching on the arm of Leigh's chair, he eyed his stepsister knowingly. "I'll bet you've been up to your old tricks."

Leigh barely heard the family banter. She was too busy trying to cope with the intimacy of her position. Joshua was behaving as though they were friends of long standing. His arm was draped over her shoulders, a heavy warmth holding her near without imprisoning her. It was unbelievably easy to lean back and allow the Dancer family to pull her into its midst. Later she would probably regret her lack of resolve where Joshua was concerned, but for now she intended to enjoy the situation in which she found herself.

"I have not been complaining about being flat on my back. I haven't mentioned my knitting either," Missy shot back indignantly. "I've been lying here like a good little mama-to-be and minding my doctor's orders." She glanced at her husband for support. "Tell him, honey."

"I haven't heard a peep out of her," Ray agreed with a wink that included Leigh.

Missy aimed a mock glare at her spouse. "Darling, did you say you missed my cooking?"

Ray's face fell with ludicrous rapidity. "You wouldn't," he pleaded, recognizing the threat.

"Wouldn't I?" Brown eyes promised retaliation for his defection.

Groaning, Ray held up both hands in surrender. "I've been living off hamburgers for two days and it'll be a week before I can get our stuff unpacked enough to find the kitchen things."

"And my knitting. I'm right in the middle of a baby sweater."

"You're always right in the middle of one project or another," Joshua pointed out dryly before glancing down at Leigh. "The day Missy married Ray was the happiest moment of my life. Now she has someone else to knit for besides me."

Leigh chuckled at his pained expression and its subsequent triumphant satisfaction. For a split second something dark and vibrant flared to life in Joshua's eyes. Then in a blink it was gone, leaving a daring grin on his lips. Looking hurriedly away, Leigh focused on Missy's face.

"Have you ever thought of selling your work?"

Surprised, Missy stared at her for a moment then asked, "Me? You can't be serious. Everyone on the floor has been saying how special all the artisans are that work for you. I don't think I could possibly qualify." She frowned, suddenly struck by another possibility. "Unless you weren't suggesting your shop as a buyer."

"Actually I was thinking of my shop."

Leigh grinned slightly at the immediate look of relief on Missy's face. She was as transparent as spring water in her reactions. For an instant Leigh envied her the innocence that allowed her the privilege.

"I'm always looking for new craftsmen and women." She was a little surprised at the offer of work she was extending. As Joshua's stepsister, Missy probably wanted for nothing.

Missy hesitated, obviously thinking the suggestion over. "I'd really like to do it," she admitted at length. "But what about the baby? I have no idea how much time I'll have once he's born. Besides, I'm still not sure I'd be good enough."

Joshua leaned over to raise one leg of his slacks to display dark socks with an intricate design woven in. "That's not the work of an amateur," he pointed out.

Leigh knowledgeably assessed the professional quality of the knitting. One brow rose in approval. "For work like that I'll make an exception in quantity," she decided, lifting her eyes in time to catch the look of pleasure and awe on Missy's face.

"Do you mean it?"

"Honey, are you sure you're up to it?"

"Of course she means it."

"Just let me know when you're ready to start."

Remarks tumbled over each other creating a chaotic babble. Then a silence fell that was born of the awkwardness of each of them interrupting the other.

"Really? For sure?" Missy smiled shyly as she spoke.

Leigh nodded, laughing softly. The simplicity and unfeigned delight of youth was refreshing. Once she'd had it too. As quickly as the thought was born, she shrugged it away. The visit was going too well for her to allow dark memories to intrude.

"Let me know when you've got five or six things ready and I'll put you on the payroll."

Beside her, Joshua rose to his feet, unobtrusively urging Leigh to follow suit. "Now, young lady, Leigh and I are going so you can get some rest. See that you make use of it," he commanded, dropping his arm from Leigh's shoulders long enough to give Missy a goodbye kiss.

Missy wrinkled her nose in a saucy gesture that did nothing to disguise the affection in her eyes. "Yes, brother dear," she agreed with suitable, though clearly faked, meekness.

Ray shook his head, exchanging a look with Leigh. "Pay no attention. They're always like this."

One brow rose at his confidence. "And you love every minute of it," she couldn't resist saying. For an instant she wondered if that was really she taking part in the lively repartee. When was the last time she enjoyed herself so wholeheartedly?

"Ready, Leigh?"

Joshua's voice drew her attention. Ebony eyes, full of curiosity, watched her intently as she blinked away the unfamiliar mental questions. It had been too long since she had thought about something as simple as having fun. "If you are," she responded as lightly as she was able.

Joshua took her hand, slipping his fingers between hers before she had a chance to protest at yet another casually intimate gesture. A few steps brought her the privacy of the hallway but not a release.

"Joshua?" Leigh wiggled her fingers while keeping pace with his long strides.

He glanced at her as he allowed her to precede him into the conveniently empty elevator. "Not here, Leigh."

Leigh stared at him in surprise. "What?" she demanded, completely at sea to his meaning.

His jaw tightened at her blank expression, his lashes dropping to shield the thoughts reflected in them. He had to know what haunted her, what terrors a hospital held for her. A woman with her courage didn't have panic in her eyes for no reason.

"I need to understand your ghosts."

Her eyes widened at the quietly given statement. "I don't have any ghosts," she began in an automatic defense, only to be silenced by a harshly disbelieving look. "And if I did—" Leigh broke off abruptly when the elevator doors slid noiselessly open to reveal a small crowd in the lobby waiting to board. Without another word, Leigh accompanied Joshua out of the elevator, through the common area and into the sunshine-painted landscape and the parking lot beyond.

"We've been through this before," she reminded him quickly.

"Agreed. But I think you need to tell someone. I'm here and I care. Think of it as a small installment on what I owe you if you like."

Leigh didn't know what to say. On the one hand she hated being reminded of the debt Joshua mistakenly thought he owed her. On the other hand she could not help but be touched by his caring. The emotions both responses created were too vivid to be comfortable. Control she understood, but this carousel of feeling was more than she wanted or intended to cope with. Before she could frame a suitably off-putting reply she found herself gently stuffed into Joshua's car and on her way home.

"How do you know I haven't told anyone?" Leigh got out finally, curious in spite of herself.

Joshua glanced at her then back to the road, shrugging in a gesture designed to mean anything. "You're the most solitary person I've ever met. And I know you're a strong woman. You wouldn't share your problems." He frowned, his gambler expression showing an uncharacteristic hint of uncertainty. "And before you ask, I have no idea why it's so important to me to be the one you do talk to. I have never badgered any one in my life the way I have you the last days."

Amazed at his accurate pinpointing of her thoughts, Leigh's lips parted in astonishment. "So you do know what you have been doing," she murmured after a moment.

"Of course I do." He gave her a quick look. "I've tried to be patient, you know. It hasn't worked. One, because I am basically a doer type."

"And two?" Leigh prompted when he didn't say any more.

"And you are too private for words. I feel like I have to dig for every piece, every thought. Nothing with you is what it seems."

"I'm not sure I like that description," she mused, eyeing him. Her wariness was increasing with each statement.

Joshua chuckled, flicking her a quick look. "Why not? Too much feminine mystique for you?"

"Well, now that you mention it," she drawled. "No woman likes to be that unpredictable."

Joshua swung the car into her driveway behind the dark gray pickup the garage had finally seen fit to return. "Unpredictable? Lady, you invented the word," he muttered, eyeing the gleaming, gun-metal machine ahead with sudden irritation. "And turned it into a fine art."

The abrupt mood switch stole the relaxed expression from Leigh's face. "Joshua," she warned, protesting his return to the subject she had momentarily forgotten was at hand.

The lapse unsettled her. She had no excuse for the temporary loss of memory. No excuse except for Joshua's potent male charm and freewheeling exercise of it. She'd never met a man so adept at slipping in and out of verbal corners. He seemed to call up, with little effort, the emotions she had long controlled. His touch was feather light and deft, leaving her stranded time and again on some invisible rocky plateau from which he'd then ease her gently back to smoother ground. And damn him, she had yet to find a way of stopping him.

"Coming?" Joshua queried.

Leigh turned her head to find Joshua waiting beside the open door, his eyes challenging her to refuse to ask him in. Leigh slipped gracefully from the car, accepting the dare with a lift of her chin. They both knew she was playing into his hands and the knowledge galled her even as it made her all the more determined that this time she'd come out the victor or, at least, not the loser, she decided with grim humor. Unlocking the front door, she bent to greet Dutch. She was aware Joshua watched her every move. When she rose, her face was wiped clean of every emotion. When one played poker with the best of the riverboat men, one kept the cards close to one's chest.

"The living room?"

Joshua nodded once, accepting the place. Admiration shone briefly in his eyes as she passed him to lead the way. His gaze followed her, tracing her slender shape as she stopped at the window, her back to him. Rejection was in her stance but there was pride too. The tilt of her head said what her lips would not, *You are intruding. I will not give way this time.*

For a moment he again wondered why he pushed into areas she obviously wanted left inviolate. Then the memory of her bleak eyes, the vulnerable reaction in the parking lot before they had gone in to see Missy reminded him of the causes if not the reasons.

"Save us both this and tell me why the visit began the way it did."

"No." Leigh focused on the daffodil bed she'd weeded the week before in an effort to remind herself of where she was. Bright sunshine-yellow blossoms waved gently in the breeze, offering silent encouragement.

Joshua sighed, running his fingers through his hair at the only course left open to him. "You were shaking with nerves when we got there. I'll grant you that you hid it well."

It was true. She didn't even wonder how he had detected her mental state. Knowing, in this case, held more of a threat than ignorance. She waited for the rest of his questions. Maybe she'd add iris to the garden next. The vivid purple would be a nice counterpoint.

"What is it about Missy that bothers you?"

Leigh just stopped herself from starting and betraying how close he was to the real problem. "Maybe I have a phobia about hospitals."

"No way."

At the swiftly given certainty of his answer, Leigh swung around. "Then you tell me," she challenged, taking the offensive out of his hands.

Joshua frowned, staring at her, trying to penetrate the barrier she'd erected. "It's not hospitals. At least not the whole of it."

She tipped her head, feeling almost euphoric with the success of her attack. She might win after all. A second later she felt like kicking herself for being so naive.

"Then it's got to be her pregnancy. Something to do with her miscarrying." He pinned her with twin lasers of black light. "Have you lost a child?" Three steps closed the gap between them.

Leigh stood her ground, retreating neither from his conclusions nor his approach. In a sudden flash of insight she realized she could have prevented this inquest if she'd really wanted to. Joshua was no heavy-handed bully. He would have backed off if she'd been adamant. Had she wanted him to learn the truth that much? She searched his expression and found concern, empathy and understanding. What she didn't see was the rejection experience had taught her to expect.

"Yes, I carried the promise of a child in my body. A car wreck caused by a drunk snatched it from me," Leigh admitted slowly, her voice rock-steady and hiding all feeling. Most of the anger and bitterness had burned out of her, and what little remained she kept under tight wraps.

Joshua went completely still, only the faint sound of his breathing marking his existence. He hurt for her. His body was tensed against the wave of pain rolling over it. Her tone showed none of the agony she must have suffered, nor did her face betray her now. Only her eyes, haunted silver mists filled with cruel shadows, cried out in silent rage at the theft of what she had held dear. And she had held it dear, this unborn being. He knew it without asking. Her home and her business spoke of a love of family. It told of her generosity, caring and gentleness.

"Why isn't he with you?"

"Who?" Not immediately comprehending the question, Leigh forgot to guard her words.

"The man who shared the creation of life with you," Joshua elaborated roughly, forcing himself to finish what he'd started.

"He left when he found out," she said flatly. She tried to stop, but she couldn't hold back the words. She couldn't protect the peace of the new place she had built with lies. "He couldn't deal with what happened."

Joshua inhaled sharply as fury at the unknown lover shook him to the core. His hands clenched in helpless frustration. "The bastard." The words were ripped from him, a fitting epithet.

Leigh shook her head, her silver hair belling out in a soft cloud. "No, he wasn't. I had nothing to give him any more. He had nothing for me. Our marriage was as dead—" Her voice broke over the word, then reformed, empty of all but the sounds of stark letters and syllables. "As dead as our child."

Joshua closed his eyes for an instant, hating the man who had left her empty and alone when she needed him. Joshua wouldn't call him husband. He didn't deserve the title.

"I'm sorry," he whispered, aching to take her in his arms but afraid she would turn on him like a hurt and wounded creature that had been hunted too long.

"You needn't be. I survived."

"Surviving isn't living." Joshua bent until he could feel the warmth of her lightly touching his body. Close as he dared, but still avoiding the physical contact he feared she would reject. "We aren't all like him, this man you loved."

"Aren't you?"

"No."

Leigh stepped back, tired now of the inquisition she never should have permitted to happen. At least by giving Joshua this much, the greater part of her secret was protected. She could tolerate almost anything but pity. "No matter."

Straightening, Joshua allowed her to move away. He had gotten the answers that he wanted but at what cost to her? Seeing the way she held her arms wrapped around herself told part of the price she'd paid, while her eyes held an agony he suspected went far deeper than the hell she'd already shown him. Emotion, cloudy and without a name, filled his mind, confusing him about what to do now. In a few days he had gotten more involved than he'd ever intended yet he was certain he would do it all again. The surety in him shook him. Who was Leigh? How had she slipped beneath his guard so easily? He lived in a world of predictable numbers, cool logic, and more often than not, greed. She, and the attraction he felt for her, just didn't compute, not for him and obviously not for her.

But he couldn't walk away. That was the bottom line. Illogical perhaps, even stupid, but true nonetheless. His gut instinct said there was something special happening, something worth exploring.

"Please go. There's nothing for you here."

Leigh faced him, numb to any reaction except a need for privacy. She was cold, bone deep and soul wide. Shivers touched her lightly. She barely noticed.

Joshua did, a frown wrinkling his brow at her uncaring immobility. With a muffled oath he whipped the fleecy mohair afghan from the end of the couch and draped it around her shoulders shawl style.

"Sit down, Leigh, before you fall over," he commanded gruffly, guiding her to the armchair beside the fireplace.

"I'm all right. I just want you to go," she pleaded, too tired to resist him physically.

He pushed her gently back against the cushion, raising her head with a finger beneath her chin. "I'll leave as soon as I'm sure you're all right. Do you have any brandy?"

"No."

"Tea, I guess," he decided, tucking the knitted cover snugly around her quivering limbs. Trailing a forefinger lightly down her cheek, Joshua smiled soothingly. "Stay put while I make it."

Leigh's gaze followed him out of the room, her mind blank. It was as if every thought and emotion had been emptied out of her by a giant hand. She felt as bare as the hearth beside which she sat. She couldn't even question why Joshua was still there. She just didn't care. When he returned with two steaming mugs, she took the one he offered her without comment. They drank in silence, he kneeling beside her and she wrapped in a cocoon of delicate handiwork.

"More?" he asked on seeing her finish the last swallow.

"No."

Joshua took the cup and placed it next to his on a nearby table. Rising, he studied her downcast head for a long moment without speaking. "I'm coming back to town next weekend. Have dinner with me on Friday."

"No."

"Why not?"

Prodded by his relentless pursuit, Leigh looked up. "I don't want to."

"What you mean is, you're afraid." he argued bluntly. "You want to hide and I'm not going to let you do it."

"You can't stop me."

"Want to bet?"

"No." Leigh drew back quickly when he bent down, an arm on each side of her, trapping her in place.

His expression tightened at the involuntary flinch, his mouth a grim, twisted slash. "Don't ever do that again. Not with me. I wouldn't touch you in anger, not ever." Joshua clenched his jaw, striving to control the flash of temper. An outburst now was the last thing she needed.

"I'll pick you up at seven. Wear something pretty." Black eyes stared into slate gray. Challenge meeting the beginnings of defiance.

"And if I'm not here?" Unaware of the small gesture, Leigh tilted her chin.

Joshua caught the flash of spirit with a deep sense of relief. He had meant to nudge her temper and succeeded. "You'll be here if for no other reason than to sling a pot at my head," he returned, dropping a fleeting kiss on her lips before she could protest. He grinned at the glare she gave him. "Make that two pots."

"How about a cast-iron skillet?" she muttered as he headed for the door.

"If you think you can handle it."

The male taunt floated over his shoulder with a lusty chuckle. He neither hesitated nor looked back before he left. Leigh stared after him, so caught up in deciding on a suitable way to take him down a peg that she forgot the emptiness that had stolen her spirit for a moment. Fighting her way out of the suddenly stifling folds of the afghan, she marched to the kitchen with the faithful Dutch at her heels. Releasing the keeshond for his run, she stared around the room seeking an inspiration.

"That overbearing man. I'll show him. Pick you up at seven! Pretty! Humph!" The unladylike sound followed her into the bedroom where it punctuated various other mutterings. She fell into bed to dream of a sloe-eyed gambler fleeing from a platinum-haired creature in a flaming temper. Closer and closer she came—the skillet she brandished flashed overhead—it came down in a swinging arc—at the last second he turned and smiled.

Leigh caught her breath and jerked upright in bed. "Damn that man! I can't even murder him in my sleep!"

Six

———

Leigh sipped her tea, eyeing the morning newspaper with a decided lack of interest. "What's good about Wednesdays, Dutch? They're just the middle of the week. Three more days to go until a day off."

The keeshond poked his black muzzle under her arm, brown-gold eyes staring at her out of a wolf's face.

"Quite a conversationalist, aren't you, my friend?" She patted his head before draining the last of the first cup of morning tea and getting to her feet. The house was too quiet today. Even the birds were silent. Where was everyone? Joshua was in—

She hauled her thoughts to a screeching halt, having promised herself, in the wee hours of a restless night, that she wouldn't think of him. It was bad enough that he had invaded her dreams four nights in a row.

Missy. The younger woman was far less troublesome to consider, to wonder about. What was Missy doing today? Knitting? Leigh frowned at the thought. No, she wasn't doing that unless Ray had managed to unpack already. Leigh had noticed the moving van on Monday at their house at the end of the street.

Suddenly the word *unpack* made its significance known. When Missy and Ray had been discussing their household arrangements during that horrible race to the hospital, she had other things on her mind. Things like how to arrive in one piece had seemed more important than a conversation designed to take Missy's mind off her aching body. Now every word was coming back to Leigh with startling clarity.

The couple had purchased the small house on Dogwood, as their first real home, with the money Missy's brother had given them as a wedding present for a down payment. At the time Leigh could remember thinking how generous the brother sounded. Now she realized why. Joshua was a wealthy, caring man, while his sister and her husband seemed determined to stand on their own feet and not live off his largess. It was a measure of the determination of both sides that they had worked out a compromise.

Josh provided the down payment, a set of living-room furniture, and paid to have them moved from Nashville to Knoxville. Missy and Ray would do the moving themselves instead of allowing Josh to pay the movers to do it. Missy and Ray had seemed quite proud of themselves for having won that concession.

Ray started his new job on Monday. Today was Wednesday. If he was settling into Dancer's Knoxville branch, who was taking care of Missy? Given Missy and Ray's independence, it was entirely possible Missy was home alone. Leigh stared at the phone, silently condemning herself for not having thought of this sooner. True, she had been extraordinarily busy the past three days, often getting home after nine at night. But that was no excuse.

"But it's not my problem. I'm not her keeper," Leigh muttered, taking two steps toward the phone. "Besides I must get to work." One finger dialed information. A moment later Missy's number looked back at her from the personal directory hanging on the wall.

"Oh blast," she swore softly, giving in. Before the fourth ring Missy's breathless voice gasped a greeting.

Leigh paled at the sound, a too-vivid imagination supplying too many unpleasant reasons for her breathless condition. "Missy, it's Leigh. Are you all right?" she demanded sharply.

"Fine." Missy inhaled deeply, then tried again. "I was just trying to find the phone. It was in a drawer, of all places."

Sagging weakly against the refrigerator, Leigh groped for her composure. "How's the moving going? Is there anything I can do to help?" She frowned at the silence that followed. "Missy?"

Missy laughed shakily. "I was deciding if I dared be truthful," she confessed.

Puzzled, Leigh stared into space, curious at the undertones she detected. "Is something wrong?"

"Not exactly," Missy sighed. "It's just that Ray's hovering so much that it's driving me nuts. He wants to hire the movers to unpack and we can't afford that. And I can't stand this mess—or seeing him come home from work to no supper and crates in the living room," she blurted out with a suspicious catch in her voice. "Josh told me I should let him pay for a maid to come in and help but I told him no. Now I wish I hadn't been so hasty. But the doctor said I didn't need anyone if I took it easy, so I thought I would be all right." The disjointed sentences ended in an subdued wail of panic.

Leigh gripped the receiver, trying to decide what was best to do. Feeling ill-equipped to sort out the Dancer sense of pride, she settled on Ray's part in the situation. "Is that what Ray's been doing?" She never should have called. This kind of involvement was just what she didn't wish to risk.

"Ray's determined to take care of me." The quiet pride in Missy's tone was unmistakable. "I feel like I'm letting him down by not doing my share."

"You are doing your share by taking care of yourself and that baby you're carrying." Leigh's quick defense was almost absentmindedly given. A frown lined her brow as she considered the problem. Ray and Missy wouldn't accept help from Joshua but they might from a friend, especially if neither of them was given a choice in the matter.

"Put your feet up and stop worrying. Help is on the way."

"Leigh, what—" Missy began, only to be cut off.

"I'll see you in a bit," Leigh said and hung up. Then she dialed the store. "Sally, do you think you can handle the shop by yourself today?"

"Why? Are you sick?"

"No, I'm going to be helping Missy move in. Remember I told you they had taken that little house down the street? Well, she's there surrounded by boxes and crates and worrying about letting her husband down."

"Crazy girl," Sally retorted. "I'm surprised her brother hasn't stepped in and sent someone out there to help out."

"He tried and didn't succeed. I think those two have more pride than sense."

"I won't ask how you know that," Sally replied, then went on briskly before Leigh could comment. "I'll hold down the fort while you do your good-neighbor act. Call if I can do anything else."

Leigh replaced the receiver, her mind already caught up in planning what to take with her to Missy's. She only needed a few minutes to load the truck with cleaning supplies and to lock the house up. Then she was on her way.

Leigh couldn't help being a little shocked at her impulsiveness in taking time off. She never did that, not since the day Leigh's Country Crafts had opened its

NO COST! NO OBLIGATION! NO PURCHASE NECESSARY!

PLAY "LUCKY 7"
AND GET AS MANY AS SIX FREE GIFTS...

HOW TO PLAY:

1. With a coin, carefully scratch off the three silver boxes at the right. This makes you eligible to receive one or more free books, and possibly other gifts, depending on what is revealed beneath the scratch-off area.

2. You'll receive brand-new Silhouette Desire® novels, never before published. When you return this card, we'll send you the books and gifts you qualify for *absolutely free*.

3. And, a month later, we'll send you 6 additional novels to read and enjoy. If you decide to keep them, you'll pay only $2.24 per book, a savings of 26¢ per book. And $2.24 per book is all you pay. There is no charge for shipping and handling. There are no hidden extras.

4. We'll also send you additional free gifts from time to time, as well as our monthly newsletter.

5. You must be completely satisfied, or you may return a shipment of books and cancel at any time.

MAKEUP MIRROR AND BRUSH KIT FREE

This lighted makeup mirror and brush kit allows plenty of light for those quick touch-ups. It operates on two easy-to-replace bulbs (batteries not included). It holds everything you need for a perfect finished look yet is small enough to slip into your purse or pocket—4-⅛" X 3" closed. And it could be YOURS FREE when you play "LUCKY 7."

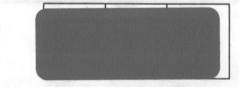

Just scratch off the three silver boxes.
Then check below to see which gifts you get.

YES! I have scratched off the silver boxes. Please send me all the gifts for which I qualify. I understand I am under no obligation to purchase any books, as explained on the opposite page.

225 CIY JAX9

NAME

ADDRESS   APT.

CITY   STATE   ZIP

7	7	7	WORTH FOUR FREE BOOKS, FREE MAKEUP MIRROR AND BRUSH KIT AND FREE SURPRISE GIFT
🍒	🍒	🍒	WORTH FOUR FREE BOOKS AND FREE MAKEUP MIRROR AND BRUSH KIT
●	●	●	WORTH FOUR FREE BOOKS
🔔	🔔	🍒	WORTH TWO FREE BOOKS

Terms and prices subject to change.
Offer limited to one per household and not valid for present subscibers.

PRINTED IN U.S.A.

DETACH AND MAIL CARD TODAY

DETACH AND MAIL CARD TODAY

BUSINESS REPLY CARD

First Class   Permit No. 717   Buffalo, NY

Postage will be paid by addressee

Silhouette Book Club
901 Fuhrmann Blvd.
P.O. Box 9013
Buffalo, NY 14240-9963

NO POSTAGE
NECESSARY
IF MAILED
IN THE
UNITED STATES

doors to the public. Why was she suddenly going out
of her way to help a woman she barely knew? Part of
the reason was the child Missy carried; that part she
knew and accepted. What she didn't understand was
the need she felt to experience the aura of caring that
surrounded Missy. Even in the sterile atmosphere of
the hospital it had been hypnotically warm and strong.
She had envied Missy her family and the closeness
with those loved ones. She had been alone so long,
first out of choice, then out of habit. Maybe she
needed to join in a family setting, even if it was only
for a little while. What could it hurt? Missy needed
help and it seemed she would not accept Josh's, so
Leigh would be doing the Dancer clan a service, or
that was what she told herself as she pulled into
Missy's driveway.

Four slender white columns and shutters adorned
the single-story brick home. Spring grass was a brilliant green carpet over the small front yard, which was
shaded by one oak and two dogwood trees. Regal ev-
ergreens in cloaks of blue-green foliage stood guard at
the entrance, while multicolored lilies, iris and daf-
fodils added a rainbow border across the front of the
house. With its peaked roof and gleaming windows,
the little house looked like a storybook cottage. Leigh
got out of the truck and went around the back to col-
lect the mop, bucket and carryall tray filled with various cleaning supplies.

A moment later she was knocking at the door. The
expression on Missy's face when she answered was a
picture of surprise, shock and downright amazement.

"But don't you work on Wednesdays?" Missy tried to protest as she was ushered by Leigh into the crate-strewn living room.

"I do and I am. Right here," Leigh glanced around, spotting an overstuffed easy chair. "I'm going to pull this into the dining area so you'll have a good view of the kitchen," she decided. "I'll start in there. Once we get those cabinets filled I bet half of these boxes will be empty. Then we'll tackle the bedroom. All you get to do is direct." She fixed Missy with a stern look. "And before you say anything, I'm doing this for that baby you're carrying. I'm not your brother, so don't bother arguing about whether I should be here or not."

Leigh's eyes held understanding and an unconscious plea for cooperation. "Everything will be just the way you want it. I promise."

Missy's brown eyes welled with tears of gratitude. Blinking rapidly, she sought to dispel the betraying moisture. A tremulous smile touched her lips as she took her place.

"I don't know what to say," she began softly.

Leigh interrupted her cheerfully, carefully concealing her relief. "You can start by telling me where you want your silverware. Right now it seems to be decorating one whole counter all by itself."

Missy laughed, the sound filling the room with delicate amusement. "I'm afraid that was Ray's doing yesterday morning. He was looking for the top to the coffeepot. He never did find it," she confided before turning to direct the placement of the first carton of dishes into the kitchen cabinets.

Leigh worked swiftly while keeping up a line of chatter with Missy. The subjects varied and helped the time and the labor pass almost without notice. She discovered Ray was starting with Dancer Investments since he had just finished college. That the baby had been a surprise, but a welcome one. Missy and Ray had been married three years and every one of them was spent poor, struggling but happy despite Joshua's repeated attempts to help out. The last announcement held that Dancer pride Leigh had come to expect. Reading between the lines, she also glimpsed a picture of Joshua's understanding and silent support of their do-it-alone policy.

Leigh found herself more drawn to Joshua with each revelation. There was so much to like about him. The man had style, class and the kind of sensitivity she admired. He also had good taste in furniture she decided later that afternoon as she surveyed the now neat, uncluttered rooms approvingly. The last of the knickknacks had just been placed on the tables. The linen closet was done, the bedroom and bath in apple-pie order, the kitchen and dining room were also finished. The second bedroom which, at the moment, was empty of everything but a stuffed, yellow- and brown-spotted giraffe, had been the last room they'd tackled. It had been the easiest, only needing vacuuming.

"I can't believe it," Missy murmured, her eyes shining with happiness. "Even the boxes are gone.

Won't Ray be surprised?'' Suddenly she sniffed the air, her expression puzzled. ''Are we cooking something?''

''There was some ground chuck in the frig and a meat-loaf recipe stuck on the cabinet, so I mixed it up and put it in the oven while you were in the shower,'' Leigh replied, shrugging slightly. ''Take-out food isn't all that good for pregnant ladies.''

''I don't know how to thank you,'' Missy began, smiling through her tears.

''Then don't. I wanted to do it.'' Leigh backed up a step, suddenly afraid of the unconscious emotional ties snaking out to trip her up. The air was alive with feelings she hadn't used in a long time.

Missy frowned, recognizing but clearly not understanding Leigh's withdrawal. For a second neither woman spoke. Then magically, before Leigh could decide how to leave gracefully, Missy's face altered.

''I didn't think. Joshua hates it when I thank him, too. I guess I'll just have to get around you like I do him,'' she remarked, urging Leigh toward the door.

Startled, Leigh stared at her. ''What—'' she began only to be cut off.

Missy grinned mischievously. ''I promise you'll like it.'' She giggled, looking more like a teenager than a woman of twenty-one. ''He always does despite what he says.'' She rose on her toes and planted a kiss on Leigh's cheek before she could protest. ''And it won't be socks.''

With that cryptic reassurance she closed the door gently, leaving Leigh standing in the hallway with a bewildered expression on her face. Shaking her head, she sought to clear the cobwebs from her mind.

"I wonder what she's planning?" she asked herself a few moments later. She climbed into the truck, stifling a groan as her muscles complained about more unwanted activity. "The next time I get an impulse, I'm going to remember some of the drawbacks. Aching bodies and grateful people are definitely hazardous to my health."

The short drive home was an exercise in verbal reprimand. Had she thought she was in shape? Fool! Could bones hurt? Or hair? Her fingers were not only pickled but peeling from the cleaners she'd used in the bathroom. Why hadn't she remembered to take some rubber gloves? The irrelevant question brought a tired smile to her lips. What difference did it make now?

"I may not live until tomorrow," she groaned on gingerly getting out of the truck. "I may not even make it to the house."

Two hours later Leigh came downstairs after a long, hot soak in the tub. "At least I feel more human. I think I may live after all," she murmured out loud as she eased down onto the sofa in the study.

Dark paneling, rich colors and books of all kinds created a warm, relaxing environment. The soft melodic strains of a classical guitar drifted from the stereo to soothe her senses much as the hot bubble bath had pampered her tired body. A light supper followed by a steaming pot of her favorite peppermint tea, enjoyed in the privacy of her hideaway, was the perfect finish for a very satisfying day. Relaxing on the couch, she let music surround her while she sipped the spicy brew.

Suddenly the phone rang, disrupting the peace and causing Leigh to spill the tea. Quickly putting the offending cup on the tray, she reached for the receiver with one hand while dabbing with a napkin at the damp spots on her caftan with the other. A second shock awaited her in the identity of her caller.

"Joshua," she breathed in surprise, all motion ceasing.

"Did I wake you?"

How could a voice be so filled with emotion and depth, Leigh wondered vaguely as the liquid-smooth cadence flowed through her. Warm, intimate, deep with masculine assurance, it bewitched even as it beguiled.

"No, you didn't wake me," she replied more to break the silence than anything else.

"Did I catch you at a bad time?"

"No." He ought to be illegal, and, considering the way he sounded, immoral.

Joshua sighed audibly. "Why do I get the feeling I'm carrying on this conversation with myself?"

"I don't know." Brilliant Leigh! Where are your brains? Making a determined effort to pull herself together, Leigh took a deep breath and reminded herself that Joshua was just a man.

"Actually I was just having a pot of tea before calling it a night," she explained on a more rational level. "Why?"

It was Joshua's turn to hesitate. How did he say thank you to a woman who made it crystal clear she didn't like gratitude. "I just finished talking to Missy and Ray..." he began.

Leigh groaned softly, shutting her eyes wearily as she leaned back against the cushions. "Not you, too."

"Yes, me too." He had no trouble following her meaning. Missy had thought it interesting that Leigh was so like him. "I appreciate what you did today," he said firmly before continuing on a more rueful note. "It's a damn sight more than I was able to do. Those kids have cornered the market on pride and self-reliance. They hardly let me help them at all."

Despite her best intentions Leigh couldn't control a grin at his very real indignation. Affection and admiration were poor substitutes for the obvious concern he had for Missy's health.

"To tell you the truth I wasn't sure Missy was going to let me help," she confessed impulsively.

"How did you manage to get past her?"

"I cheated. I didn't tell her what I had in mind." She shared his appreciative amusement.

"Why didn't I think of that?"

"I've always said women have more guile than men." Enjoying the repartee, Leigh curled comfortably into the pillows and picked up her mug again.

"Female chauvinist," he accused.

"Realist."

"Does that mean I've got to guard my flank?"

"Not unless you're planning to attack." Had she really said that? The sudden silence between them confirmed she had.

Joshua exhaled slowly, his voice dropping to an intimate drawl that sent shivers down Leigh's spine.

"Then I guess I'd better brush up on my battle strategy."

There were a dozen excuses Leigh could have given herself for the way she was acting. She was tired. It was late and she was more vulnerable at night than any other time. None were the truth. A coward she might be by some people's judgment. But dishonest, she wasn't.

Whether she had been waiting for Joshua to call she wasn't certain. What she did know was that excitement she had once promised herself she wouldn't feel was a fire in her blood. Danger sang a siren's song to her senses. Reason whispered softly in her mind, then gave up when she refused to listen.

"I hope you're a quick study."

Joshua chuckled, his amusement rich and full-bodied. "You're challenging me, spitfire."

Was she? She needed her head examined, she decided while she silently admitted he was right. "Not challenging. Protecting myself."

Joshua caught the slight withdrawal but ignored it. She'd given herself away and he wasn't about to forget it. "I think our date Friday is going to be very interesting."

Leigh heard the eager anticipation he made no effort to hide. It probably matched hers, although she wasn't about to tell him that. "We'll see."

"You're beginning to sound cautious again, so I'll say good-night," Joshua murmured huskily. "See you Friday, Lady Leigh."

Before Leigh could argue over his arbitrary ending of the conversation, she heard the dial tone. "Blast that man," she exclaimed, glaring at the receiver as she replaced it. She hadn't meant to have one blessed thing to do with the infuriating creature after the date he'd maneuvered her into and now this. Had she really engaged him in a verbal duel? She had to have been out of her mind. Frowning at her own inexplicable behavior, Leigh rose and padded upstairs to bed.

And the worst part of the whole thing was that she'd enjoyed every minute of the exchange. She liked crossing swords with Joshua. He was stimulating, interesting and too attractive for her peace of mind. She even liked his family. Why shouldn't she, a little voice demanded as she plumped the pillow. They were open, friendly and caring. In a nutshell, they were nice!

Nice? Joshua? Who was she kidding? Bold. Daring. Sexy and more exasperating than any male had a right to be. But he touched her quiet world with fiery color, flashing lights and a cacophony of sound. He made her senses sing again when she'd thought them mute.

"Good night, gambler man," she whispered in the darkness. A tiny smile curved her lips as she closed her eyes to sleep.

Seven

Leigh walked in the early evening shadows, her gaze drifting from Dutch to the serene paths in the backyard garden. The skirt of the silk dress she wore danced gently around her legs. A light breeze teased the branches overhead and the small flowering plants at her feet. Anticipation sang an intoxicating melody in her mind. It had driven her to dress early and, ultimately, to seek the tranquility of the outdoor oasis she'd planted.

A car purred in the distance, coming closer. His? She froze, a slender statue clothed in a mauve-rose gown. Dutch barked once before charging down the path that led to the drive. Still she didn't move. She was as taut as a violin string wound too tight. Part of her wanted to hide in the velvety shadows but another part needed to breathe again. To know joy and to feel alive once more. Try as she might she'd been unable to decide whether being with Joshua was really what she wanted. At the moment she seemed incapable of backing away. For the first time in her life she had no answers, only a confusion of feelings. Inhaling deeply, she took one hesitant step then another, her eyes focused on the narrow walkway ahead.

A second later Joshua was there, filling the empty place where only insubstantial shadows had been. "Leigh."

Her name whispered on the breeze, calling her to him. Her feet, encased in a web of delicate gold straps, carried her nearer. His hand came out, steady and warm, an open invitation which she almost accepted. Sanity returned just before her fingers lay in his. She jerked back. She would not give into this madness so easily. He was not a lover, perhaps not even a friend.

"How did you know I would be back here?" she demanded quickly, needing to cover up the slip she had nearly made. It was harder to ignore his disappointed expression as he dropped his hand to his side.

"I heard Dutch bark. It's a beautiful night." He shrugged. He studied her in the soft glow of the colored lights spotted above the garden. "I wasn't sure you'd be home tonight."

"I wasn't sure I'd be here, either." The admission slipped out quietly. Leigh was neither surprised nor worried she had made it. She had no idea where this relationship he seemed intent on fostering would go.

But one thing she did know was that it would not be based on lies or coy evasions.

Joshua nodded but Leigh couldn't tell what he was thinking. For a moment she wished for better light and a far less romantic setting. Speaking in hushed tones while surrounded by the near darkness and the sweet scent of the night flowers was not the way to keep a clear head.

"Why did you help Missy with unpacking?" he asked bluntly.

Leigh didn't hesitate. "Why not? It didn't really take that long. Besides she needed someone and that pride of theirs was stopping you."

"It seems out of character for a loner. Or are you changing your mind about that part of your life?"

Leigh froze. He was quick, too quick. Her first impulse was a swift denial. Fortunately she caught herself in time. "I'm not as much of a fanatic as you're implying."

"Aren't you?" he returned dryly.

Leigh lifted her chin, her eyes stormy with the beginnings of temper. "You're pushing." The warning was given in a neutral voice. The look that accompanied it was anything but.

"Not really. I'm curious about you." There was no apology or remorse in his response. He had stated the simple truth. "It's a funny thing about my business. Word gets around about a lot of things and people, too. You, lovely lady, have quite a reputation in this town."

As quickly as it had come, Leigh's irritation died as amazement drove everything else from her mind. "I do?"

He inclined his head. "Do you want to know what it is?"

"No." Her refusal was swift and starkly to the point. "I'd much rather have the dinner you promised me," she replied in an obvious attempt to change the subject.

Joshua laughed softly, catching her by surprise. "Food it is." He opened the gate and stepped into the garden with her.

When he took her hand and tucked it into the crook of his arm before she realized his intention, she did nothing more than stiffen for an instant. She gave in out of sheer necessity, or at least that's what she told herself. Struggling or demanding release would have been undignified in the extreme.

Neither spoke as she locked up the house. Joshua watched her every move, a practice that was becoming an unnerving habit with him. Leigh found it impossible to relax despite the easy flow of conversation Joshua initiated on the way to the restaurant. She was at odds with herself. Should she push him away or allow nature to guide her? Opening herself to the world again was one thing. Allowing a relationship to develop where she could be hurt was another. Even if Joshua were offering a commitment she would be equally at sea. The seesaw of her emotions annoyed her. But there didn't seem to be a thing she could do about the way she felt.

Dinner was delicious, the wine chilled, the steak medium rare just the way she liked it. Conversation flowed as easily as the vintage. Music beckoned and they danced. Yet, not once, did Joshua touch her in any way she could have objected to. There were no subtle innuendos, no delicate passes, no hands straying accidentally to set fire to her senses. Joshua was a gentleman in an old-world way she had thought no longer existed.

Thrown off balance by his restrained handling, Leigh studied him through her lashes while he drove back to her house. There was a waiting quality about him tonight, a kind of tenseness she found difficult to define.

"What's wrong?" The words in her mind emerged unplanned, a throaty whisper to betray her unease.

Joshua glanced at her briefly. One sable brow winged upward at the abrupt demand. "What makes you think there's anything wrong?" he asked in turn.

"Why do you answer a question with a question?" She saw the flash of white in the glow of the street lights and knew he smiled. It was a gesture natural to him and one often used, she suspected, to throw his opponents off guard.

"Tricks of the trade."

Leigh gave him a mild glare. "I'm not one of your moneyed clients so you can put the tricks back in the bag and give me a straight answer," she challenged firmly.

Joshua looked at her for a long second before returning his attention to his driving. "Are you sure this is what you want?"

Leigh recognized the strange, almost pleased note in his voice and wondered at it. She flicked him a glance, suddenly wary. Something had changed. The air around them was alive with unspoken messages. Danger invaded the atmosphere, like faint unseen wisps of sulfur to warn of hazards ahead. Sparks flashed behind dark eyelashes and her chin tilted as she braced herself to face the invisible perils.

"Yes."

The single word hung in the silence as Joshua drove into the driveway and stopped the car. Turning, he studied her intently. The lantern in the front yard cast an eerie shadow over his features. Never had the reckless courage in his face and the bold angle of his head been so evident. Untamed but quiet, it lay in wait for the weak, the fainthearted. Leigh was neither and she knew it.

Joshua debated lying. He couldn't do it. Even if dishonesty had been his way, Leigh wasn't a woman to be lied to. "I want you. I have almost from the first but you've made it clear you don't want a man in your life. I'm trying to remember that and it hurts like hell. I want to hold you in my arms and make exquisite love to you until neither of us can think straight."

He had to touch her. Those pale eyes of hers looked so stunned as she sat there staring at him as though he had lost his mind. Maybe he had. God knows no woman had ever affected him so strongly before. He wanted to hold her but he settled for taking her hand in his.

"You've been badly hurt. I understand that. I also know that until I came along you were safe in your little niche. I want to ask you to come out, to hold on to me and to trust me." He watched her intently, seeing the rejection in the bleakness of her eyes. "I'm asking more than you can give." The realization was a harsh whisper.

"Why, Joshua? You could have any number of women."

"So could any man or woman for that matter. There are a lot of singles running around."

She ignored the truth and concentrated on her need to know. She had to understand why he pursued her. How could she give trust without understanding? "Why me?"

The one question he couldn't answer, and she had to ask it. "I could give you words, and they wouldn't mean a thing to either of us, not really. Only you can decide if I'm like the others in your life who have let you down." Using the hand he held, he pulled her closer. "Give me a chance. That's all I ask. I want to give to you, share with you, not take. Let me be alone with you, 'Solitaire.'"

Leigh tilted her head, hair flowing down her back in a glittering cascade. A demand she could have turned aside. A plea whispered in the darkness, a voice husky with a man's honest need for her stripped her of her defenses. "I'm afraid."

"Do you think I'm not?" Joshua wrapped his arms around her, supporting and protecting her at the same time. "It's never mattered this much to me before."

"No ties. No promises." The thought of any emotional strings was more than she could bear. If she came to him it would be in a physical sense only. For both their sakes he had to understand that.

Joshua shut his eyes against the demand. She was offering him what he had enjoyed without a qualm with many women. He wanted more from her, and knew he'd lose her unless he settled for less.

"No ties. No promises," he repeated finally, each word drawn out. He felt her relax fully against him for the first time. It was almost worth the sacrifice for this much.

"Will you come in?" Leigh spoke the words against his heart.

"I'd like to very much, but you don't have to do this." He eased her away from his chest. "Are you sure?"

"Yes."

Joshua leaned forward to brush her lips lightly. It took willpower not to draw her into his arms and show her with more than words what he felt. Only the knowledge she'd retreat imposed any restraint.

"Take my hand?" he managed lightly, extending it palm up.

Leigh placed her fingers in his. Laughing a little as he tugged her across the seat so she could get out on his side, she teased him.

"It might have been easier if you had walked around."

He grinned, swinging their clasped hands between them. The relief of her acceptance made him feel young again. "But not half as much fun," he countered, his gaze going to the deep plunge at the neckline of her dress.

"Joshua Dancer, that's a sneaky trick," Leigh shot back, glaring at him when she realized what he meant.

Chuckling, Joshua hugged her close while she tried to get her hand free. If she wouldn't allow him to be serious, then he would play a little. "You might as well stop wiggling around. I'm not letting you go."

"For two cents I'd whack you one."

Twin brows inched up in curiosity. "With what?"

"This for starters," she suggested tartly, waving her soft clutch purse under his nose like a weapon.

Joshua lazily plucked the square from her grasp. "Honey, you're easy to tease and so much fun." He laughed before flipping the handbag open with familiar intimacy and extracting the key.

"Humph."

As a reply it wasn't much, but it was the best Leigh could do. Hands on hips—at least he'd released her—she stared at him, suddenly realizing his teasing had come at an extremely odd moment. It wasn't the first time either.

"You did that on purpose," she accused, unsure whether she was comfortable around a man so attuned to her needs.

He opened the door, urging her through while totally ignoring her stance. "Sure I did," he agreed as he turned to face her. "It was either that or start something you might not be ready to finish. Even if you were, I'm too old for making out on the front porch or in a car."

Dumbfounded, Leigh found herself at a loss for words. "Are you always so blunt? Or am I just privileged?"

Joshua frowned thoughtfully. "Both I think. I've played man-woman games until I'm sick of the whole ritual. I like you. You've got style, beauty, brains and more courage than is good for you." He shrugged, although his eyes were far from indifferent. "I don't want to give to you what I've given the other women in my life."

The warmth, the purpose in his voice was more than she wanted to handle coming on the heels of what had gone before. "Don't do this," she commanded, feeling hunted.

Closing the distance between them, he asked, "Don't do what? Tell you how special you are? Tell you how I respect and admire your uniqueness enough to be honest? What part don't you want to hear?" With each question he came a step nearer until he stood only a few inches away.

"I'm not like that, at all," she protested. "I'm anything but brave."

Their eyes met for a long moment. Twin breaths mingled in the silence. "Aren't you? I feel the need to retreat in you, but you haven't moved an inch." He smiled slowly, his face gentling. "Every time I advance, you stand and face me. I know men who wouldn't do that." Lifting his hands, he cupped her chin in his palms. "That fool who left you had no idea what he was giving up. You've got more to offer a man than I think you even know."

At the mention of Buddy's rejection, Leigh stiffened. But before she could move or pull away, Joshua's lips covered hers. The walls of loneliness of her self-imposed exile cracked along the tiny fissures Joshua had already created. Warmth seeped into the center of her being as she absorbed the feel of his long body against hers. Without being aware of it, she sighed. Her hands slid around his neck to thread through the velvet thickness of his hair.

Joshua kissed her as if it were the first time, gently, tenderly, his passion held in check by the strength of his promise to her.

Neither was prepared for Leigh's response, the instantaneous surge of sheer desire. A need greater than any she had ever known raced through her, pulsating with a wild, untamed rhythm. The emptiness she had carried for so long was filled with emotions too new to name. With the depth of her need came the fear that she could not satisfy him, that he would ultimately demand more than she could give and that once he touched her he would cease to want her. She forgot the fear, forgetting the man who held her.

Control sliding from his grasp, Joshua's kiss deepened far beyond what he'd intended. Sanity waged a fleeting battle with desire and lust. A groan rose from the deepest part of him to emerge as a husky word. His mouth slanted across hers, claiming the softness and taste of her as though he would never get enough. He put his arms around her blindly. It was then he felt the tension in her body and recognized that desire was not its cause. He lifted his head.

"Leigh, what is it?"

She stared at him. Suddenly she wanted someone to hold her, to keep the demons at bay. Joshua was there. He wanted her. "Make love to me."

His eyes held hers, his features taut. Something was very wrong. There was no passion in those eyes, only desperation. Tension knotted his stomach as his hand brushed across her breast. No change, no response. He knew then that he could have been anyone. He pulled away from her.

"I won't be used," he bit out harshly. "Not even by you. I've given you honesty; don't give me a lie."

Leigh drew back, feeling as though she'd been slapped. She wanted to protest. She couldn't when he only spoke the truth. "Forgive me," she whispered. Pain blazed in his eyes, pain she had put there without thought. Hating what she had done she reached out to him. He backed away.

"No more, Leigh. Not tonight. I still want you. Touch me now and I won't care why you give yourself to me." He turned to leave.

"Please stay."

He stopped, his back to her. Had she really said it...? "I don't want you out of anything but desire, passion. No guilt. No pity. No lies."

Leigh watched his rigid back. It looked as unyielding as his voice sounded. "I want you."

"Are you sure?"

"Yes."

He turned back to her then, his eyes searching hers for the truth. Neither spoke. Leigh, because she was afraid he wouldn't finish what he had begun. Joshua, because he was afraid she would slip away from him even as he held her in his arms. Leigh waited for him to come to her. When he didn't she knew he wouldn't. This time the first move was up to her. She swallowed hard before she took the first step. The second was marginally easier. The third brought her within touching distance. His hands were there waiting for her. They pulled her into his arms, his sigh warming her ear as he cradled her against him.

The first kiss was tentative, but only for a second. Leigh, having made her decision, took what he offered and demanded more. Joshua's control disintegrated. It had been tried too much in too short a space of time.

Lips imprisoned, Leigh felt herself floating, muscled arms lifting her. She was dimly aware that they were going up the stairs to her bedroom, where a single lamp cast a golden glow over the bed. Joshua set her on her feet, his fingers releasing the zipper at the back of her dress. The soft fabric fell away from her body. The cool breeze from the open window caressed her heated flesh while she worked the buttons of his shirt free. Her eyes opened fully to drink in his male symmetry while he shrugged out of his clothes.

Desire doubled, tripled and erupted when their eyes met.

A sudden stillness came without warning, an abrupt cessation of all movement except the rapid ebb and flow of dual breathing.

"Be sure, Leigh," Joshua said hoarsely. "I won't be able to stop this time."

Driven by an ancient knowledge, old as time itself, Leigh lifted her arms to him. "I'm sure."

With those two simple words, the spell was broken. He went to her, a strong man made vulnerable by a woman. His lips, hot and seeking, caressed her shoulder, throat and lips as he laid her down upon the bed. Her skin was living satin beneath his touch.

"You're beautiful," Joshua whispered roughly. He had to stroke her, now, the whole night long if she would allow it.

Leigh arched into his tantalizing caresses, her own hands searching out and molding the rippling muscles of his back and shoulders. Feverishly, her breath in small gasps, she learned the secrets of what drove him wild in her arms and what made him purr with pleasure.

Fiery, shivering tension spun a web about her until no part of her remained free. Her body twisted, arched and retreated beyond her command. His tongue swirled erotically over her breasts to the soft fullness on her belly, feeding the voracious need driving her.

Had she died, Leigh wondered dimly? The sheer pleasure flowing over her was heaven. It had to be. Nothing could top this.

Then she gasped his name. She was still here, still breathing. "Stop! Don't stop!" The command passed through her lips frantically. The pounding of her heart deafened her and she burned from head to toe.

Joshua's face was taut as he rose above her. In that moment Leigh looked into the eyes of a stranger, a being her fire and passion had created. For a split second she knew fear of his possession. And then it was gone, swept away by a fleeting whisper of gentleness in his expression, in his touch. Leigh relaxed, and knew this moment in time was right.

Fiercely she drew him to her, guiding their union with a sure touch. Desire rose higher, compelling them to seek the glorious inferno awaiting them. Stripped of everything but that need, man and woman came together as one and found completeness. Lost once, alone, now found safe, whole... at peace.

The room might have been the scene of a storm where two survivors clung together with the awed feeling of having gone through something no being had been created to survive. They held one another, unwilling to lose the closeness, the security of contact. Drained, they rested in silence. No words marred the stillness for there was nothing either could say. Minutes flowed by as each was locked in a private place, alone yet not alone.

Leigh stared at the soft thatch of hair inches from her lips, aware something cataclysmic had occurred. Joshua had added a new dimension to the term making love and in doing so had shaken the very roots of her past. All her experience with Buddy paled beside what they had shared.

"Sorry?"

Joshua's voice rumbled from the chest beneath her cheek to capture her attention.

"Right now I'm too satisfied to think." Leigh wasn't ready to examine what she had done, not now. "What about you?"

Joshua sighed, knowing he shouldn't have asked. "I'm not sorry. You're a beautiful, giving woman."

Leigh lightly traced a whorl of hair, her eyes thoughtful but still holding the remnants of passion. "It was never like this before," she confessed, sharing what she could of herself. She suddenly wanted their coming together to be more than just physical intimacy. Because she could not give him pretty words, she offered him the truth.

Joshua rose on one elbow to stare at her, his dark eyes intent. "I'm glad for my sake but not for yours."

Surprised and curious at his reply, she asked. "Why?"

"Because you're one special lady in bed, my dear," he teased, his voice caressing her without losing an ounce of sincerity. "Men have fantasies about women like you." Never had he reached so deeply for a light reply. Never had he wanted to pour out his feelings to a woman the way he wished he dared to with Leigh.

Leigh shocked herself with a giggle. "Do they? I didn't know." Humor at a moment like this would never have been possible with her ex-husband and Leigh knew it. Gratitude for the man Joshua was, filled her. He made it easy for her to lie beside him after what they had shared and not feel the need to retreat.

He looked incredibly solemn as his forefinger traced a line from her lips to the tip of one full breast. "Well, now you do and so do I. What shall we do about it?"

"Do?" she repeated, not understanding.

"Do. As in will you see me again? Or will I wake up and find out you're a pillow and this has been a very x-rated dream?"

For the first time since Joshua had entered her life Leigh didn't rise to the bait. Instead, she recognized and understood his attempt to offer her a way out if she chose to take it. Yet there was something more, too. There was a hint of uncertainty, carefully but inadequately hidden in his eyes. He'd made it clear he wanted her to want him, even needed her desire, but he would apply no more pressure.

"I'm not a pillow, I promise you," she whispered, snuggling closer.

Joshua rolled on his back, a smile curving his lips as he drew her on top of him. "No dream. Are you sure?"

"This is reality." Leigh leaned down, her hair falling on either side of her face to veil them both beneath a silver canopy. Nibbling at his lower lip, she teased the fullness with tiny bites. "Does this feel like a dream?"

Joshua quivered beneath her, his body jerking with awakening desire. "No," he gasped while he wrapped his arms around the slender feminine form holding him a willing prisoner. "This is definitely reality, woman."

He would take what she could give. Perhaps the uncertainty of keeping her in his arms added to the desire surging through him. He didn't know for sure. No promises. No commitments. Solitaire. She was as elusive as the wind that whispered through the Smokies, as subtle as the rainbow over Laurel Falls. He held her, but he did not really have her. Maybe he never would.

For the moment he had to accept that.

Eight

I'm beat. What a week." Joshua slumped into the easy chair with a weary sigh and closed his eyes.

Leigh watched him from a few feet away. Even now she could hardly believe she had actually invited him to stay the weekend. She had missed him. She hated knowing she had, but she was too honest not to admit the truth, if only silently. Those nightly phone calls from Nashville to Knoxville certainly hadn't helped her resolve what to do about him. Now he was here, in her home.

Joshua opened his eyes and smiled at her. "I missed you," he murmured huskily.

Leigh concentrated on how tired he looked as she

tried to ignore the dart of pleasure she felt at his words. "Did you?"

He laughed softly. "I'd shock you if I told you how much." He paused to wrap his fingers around her wrist when she came to stand beside his chair. Exerting a slight downward pull, he urged her into his lap.

Leigh could have resisted but she didn't. What was the point? She wanted his arms around her. Her body was hungry for the feel of his.

"I want to hold you." He stared into her eyes, his half-shielded behind thick, dark lashes. One day she would tell him the rest of whatever in her past kept her from giving herself fully to him. One day he would touch her and not feel that momentary hesitation just before she softened against him. "Okay?"

Leigh looped her arms around his neck as she nodded. "I'd like that," she admitted throatily. He rewarded her with a kiss before tucking her head against his shoulder.

Joshua held her, savoring the feel of her in his arms. Had he pushed her too hard, he wondered, remembering the silence that had followed the announcement of his plans to come back to Knoxville for the weekend. He'd truly intended to rent a hotel room. He'd never expected her awkward, although he hoped not reluctant, offer to let him stay with her. Not that it would have mattered, for he had barely given her a chance to get the words out before he'd accepted. That had been Wednesday night. He'd half expected her to withdraw the invitation. He knew what it had cost her to make it, yet, surprisingly, she had allowed it to stand.

So here he was, for the moment, in her home and in her life.

His arms tightened unconsciously, imprisoning her against him. She had been glad to see him when he arrived. The pleasure in her eyes and smile had touched him in ways he didn't fully understand. Yet he couldn't relax. Being with her wasn't as easy as he thought it would be. She had welcomed him with a kiss that had held a desire as strong as his own. Yet...

"Leigh, I—" he hesitated. How could he ask why she had extended her hospitality? What he really wanted to know was why she had let her barriers down and shown her desire for him so clearly.

Alerted by the strange tension in his voice, Leigh raised her head. "Is something wrong?" Unease rippled through her at the searching expression on his face. She thought there had been something odd about the way he had eased her away when she had greeted him at the door. "Tell me," she prompted when he didn't respond.

"You invited me here. I didn't expect it," he murmured finally, watching her reaction carefully.

Leigh's eyes widened at his words. "And you want to know why," she guessed, recognizing the question it was obvious he was reluctant to put into words.

"You've made it clear you're self-sufficient."

"I am. Do you think having you stay makes me any less so?"

"No. But something tells me I'm the first person ever to share this house with you."

Unsettled at his probing, delicate though it was, Leigh had to get up. Her face registered her surprise when he let her go with little more than a knowing look. Going to the window, she stared out into the night.

"You are," she admitted after a long moment. "Does it matter?"

"You know it does," Joshua replied deeply, getting to his feet. The rigidity of her back warned him to respect her need to remain untouched, yet nothing short of a direct command could keep him from closing the physical distance between them.

"I like being with you. You make me feel beautiful and desirable. You have a life of your own, and you respect the one I have. We enjoyed each other Sunday. Why make it more complicated than it is?"

Hearing her refine their lovemaking to a few hours of mutual physical satisfaction stopped him dead in his tracks. What she said was logical, he realized. In fact, he'd used the same argument once or twice himself. Frowning, he tried and failed to make sense of his feeling of disappointment.

Leigh turned around in time to see his expression and misunderstand its cause. "I want to be with you. No strings. No promises. Can't you accept that?"

"Most women would want more." He touched her lips, silencing her instinctive protest. "I don't mean now especially, but some time in the future surely."

"I'm not most women," she pointed out, her lips lightly brushing the tips of his fingers. "I had it once, remember?'' For a brief instant memories of the past darkened her eyes.

Joshua caught her shoulders, his hands tight on the slender bones. ''Don't think of that creep. Don't let him hurt you any more,'' he said, struck again by the depth of anger he felt for the insensitivity of Buddy Mason.

''He doesn't hurt me any more,'' Leigh answered, staring at him in surprise as she realized she spoke the truth. ''Five years is a long time. Besides, he's married now.'' A second later she remembered the divorce he was supposedly getting.

Startled at her calm announcement, Joshua dropped his hands. ''How do you know? I got the impression when you told me about how you left Chicago and came here, that you had severed all ties.''

Leigh inclined her head, acknowledging the basic accuracy of his assumption. ''All but one friend. Jean and I grew up together and shared the same schools. We were closer than sisters, especially after my parents died. I never really fit in with my family somehow. Jean was my anchor. Her parents were more giving than my own and eventually became mine by emotional adoption,'' she explained, her tone rich with the traumatic years of her childhood and budding maturity. Focusing on Joshua's face, she saw compassion, sympathy and the dreaded pity. The first two she could tolerate, barely, the third not at all. Slamming the door on the past, she forced a smile to her lips.

"So you see, I'm not quite the loner I led you to believe. I have Jean in Chicago, and Sally and a few acquaintances here." Going on tiptoe, she brushed his lips with hers. "And for now I have you."

Joshua sucked in a breath, his fingers clenching into fists before he remembered himself and relaxed. For now. The courage and resignation in those two words made him want to wrap his arms around her and tell her that she'd always have him. But he couldn't, and not just because he was positive her pride would never accept such a vow. But also, he didn't know at this moment if he could keep his word.

"True," Joshua agreed, striving to match her mood. Tucking her arm in his, he tried to believe this was the way he wanted it. His doubts were surely a product of knowing Leigh's tragic history. Any man would be touched by her story, and even moved to feel protective in ways unknown to him.

"What's for supper? Or am I taking us out?" he asked, managing to sound casual.

"Lobster, drawn butter, baked potatoes and sour cream, and salad," Leigh enumerated as she ticked the items off on her fingers. They entered the hall where she slipped out of his hold. "Why don't you take a shower and change into something comfortable while I get the food ready?"

"You don't mind?" He stared at her in amazement. "You've worked all week too," he pointed out.

Leigh tipped her head, a curious lift to one brow. "Is this a lead into another of those *most women* statements?"

He grinned, his humor stealing some of the exhaustion from his face. "Well, you'll have to admit I'm not much of a prize at the moment."

"I didn't ask for a prize. Besides it's only a dinner." Leigh shrugged as she said it. She would not be disarmed by his pleasure. Enjoying him as a lover was far different from letting him touch her emotions.

Joshua was disappointed and tried not to show it. He had hoped for more. For a moment he had thought he'd gotten it, but her calm reply had shot that idea down in flames. Turning away he started up the stairs without another word.

Leigh wanted to follow him, wishing she could recall her words. The smile was gone from his face and the pleasure from his eyes, thanks to her comment. Had she meant to do that? It had felt so good to have someone to worry over and to cook for. Too good. Angry at herself for the hot and cold way she was blowing, she whirled around and stalked to the kitchen.

Dutch was waiting for her at the back door, and she let him out with an absentminded pat. She had to remember her role. She had never been a lover before, but it couldn't be too hard considering the number of people opting for the no-strings arrangement. All she had to keep in mind was the desire they shared, and that above all things should be easy.

In a sense it was, she discovered throughout the weekend. Joshua was all she could wish for in a lover. He was sensitive, caring, humorous, generous and challenging. He teased her until her sides ached with laughter, then loved her through the three nights they had together. When he left just after dawn on Monday, she felt alone in a way she couldn't have explained if asked.

The demands of the store had never been a more welcome diversion, and she wasted no time in getting there. When Sally arrived two hours later she had caught up on the end-of-the-month accounts and begun rearranging the stock room, a job she'd been putting off for six months.

"Good heavens! What are you up to?" Sally asked, her eyes wide with shock.

Leigh rose amid the boxes and clutter around her, her hair escaping the confines of the ponytail tied by a shoelace at the nape of her neck.

"Cleaning." She wiped a dusty hand across her forehead. The resulting wide gray streak drew a grimace from her assistant.

"That much I can see, but why today of all days?" Sally demanded, ripping a paper towel off the roll standing unsteadily on a box filled with small stuffed animals. "Here, you've got a smudge."

Thrusting the square at Leigh, she picked her way over the obstacle course to deposit her handbag in the desk drawer with Leigh's. "Did you forget you have an appointment with the accountant today? I thought you were supposed to meet him at the bank."

Leigh scrubbed the mark from her face before answering. "I didn't forget about my pet project. I've been planning this expansion for too long to let it slip my mind now."

Sally joined her, her gaze flickering over the job even as she concentrated on the discussion. "Are you excited? I know I would be. Just think of the possibilities Country Crafts II will have in Nashville. All those tours around the city bring the people out in droves. Tourists lap up the reflected glory of seeing where their favorite singing stars live and collecting souvenirs from Music City, U.S.A."

"What a cynic you are," Leigh teased, then sobered. "Let's just hope the bank approves the financing so we'll get the chance to test your theory."

Sally looked puzzled. "But surely this meeting is only a formality. With your business record how could it be anything else?"

Shrugging, Leigh tried to ignore the faint doubts about her plans and what they meant in terms of debt and demands on her time. She had wanted, worked and planned for this moment for two years. Yet now the big event was at hand she couldn't help wondering if she'd bitten off more than she could chew alone.

"The bank is slightly more conservative than I expected," she admitted finally, voicing her concern.

"What you really mean is they're leery of a woman contemplating what you have in mind." The annoyance Sally felt was clear in her comment. "If they knew you as well as I do, they'd give you the damn money and forget their idiotic questions. You live and breathe this business. And I know you've got every bolt, board and shelf planned for the Nashville store.

And three-fourths of the stock is promised and only waiting for a word to go into production."

Smiling faintly at Sally's heated defense, Leigh felt her doubts slip away. "Sometimes you remind me so much of Jean."

Sally tipped her head, curiosity displacing her irritable expression. "One of these days I've got to sit down and have a talk with that woman. It hardly seems fair that I know so much about her without ever having met her."

"You two would get along great," Leigh said, returning to the job at hand. She opened a box of cornhusk dolls and handed Sally the handwritten invoice.

Sally began checking off each item as Leigh unwrapped the miniatures, one by one. "So you have told me more than once. It's too bad Jean's finances don't stretch to taking a trip down this way."

Leigh nodded, wishing she could see her old friend and introduce her to Sally. "Maybe this year. Her husband's new business is finally taking off. She said in her last letter that since the baby is weaned and she doesn't have to put in so many hours helping Ted at the office, she just might work in a visit."

"Just remember that if she does come I am first on the list of things to see in Knoxville." She lifted her head long enough to give Leigh a stern look before asking, "What's next to unpack?"

Sighing with mock resignation, Leigh replied. "Yes, mother. I promise you will top the list of tourist attractions." She gestured to a small box on the desk. "And that is the next box of goodies."

The rest of the morning passed in its usual busy fashion. Customers, new and old, stopped in with pleasing regularity, speeding up the hours so that it was time to leave almost before Leigh knew it. The drive to the bank, where she was to meet the accountant and the loan executive to discuss the financing of the expansion, would have been relaxing in any other circumstances. Now it simply gave her ample opportunity to become aware of the screaming squadron of 727-sized butterflies lodged in her stomach. She might look the picture of calm professionalism on the outside, she decided as she surveyed her reflection in the compact mirror, inside it was definitely air-raid time.

"I will not worry. I will not worry," she mumbled, getting out of the car. "It's only a simple loan. Nothing vital. Only a store." She made it to the door of the Bearden branch office, stopped, swallowed and pushed open the glass barrier. "It's only my life!"

The cheerful calling of her name brought Leigh's head up with a snap. A smile found its way to her lips, more in an automatic gesture than one she had thought out. "Mr. Brown." She extended her hand as the officer came toward her.

"Your timing is perfect. Your accountant just arrived as I finished a meeting on your proposal." As he talked he subtly guided her toward his office.

"So soon? I thought you needed more information than we had provided the first time."

Chuckling at her surprise, he gestured her to the chair directly facing his desk. "Well, your Mr. Ward was most helpful, and since you had expressed an urgency to begin construction early, I tried to expedite things." He sat back, his soft paunch and kindly smile giving him the appearance of a benign Buddha.

"Don't look so stunned, Leigh," Jeff Ward commented, speaking for the first time since she'd come in. "It really is true."

Leigh knew she had blown whatever sophisticated image she'd tried to project, but in that second she didn't care. She'd gotten it! She'd actually done it! The knowledge was heady and sweet with the promise of the future.

The two men exchanged glances. At another time Leigh might have been annoyed at the man-to-man look. "Your building site has been approved. We'll print the checks in the next few days and you may sign the contracts." He paused, his expression turning serious for a moment. "May I say I hope this turns out as nicely for you as the plans indicate. It's been a pleasure to work with someone who not only knows what she wants but has the enthusiasm and knowledge to bring her ideas to fruition."

To say Leigh was flabbergasted would have been putting it mildly. The older man's words were obviously sincere as was the admiring look in his eyes.

She gave her thanks quietly, then spoiled the effect with a grin. "I hope they turn out that way too. I've spent two years working on this."

"It shows." The banker rose. "I suppose we could have handled this by phone, but I confess I wanted to do it in person."

Touched by the human side of the executive who, until now, had been as personable as a piece of hotel furniture, Leigh extended her hand in a gesture far warmer than their first greeting of the day.

"Somehow a phone call wouldn't have been half as satisfying," she murmured gently. Pretending not to notice the faint tinge of red creeping up his neck, she turned to Jeff. "Are you leaving too?"

He nodded before offering his goodbye. Seconds later they were outside. "I never thought I'd live to see the day," Jeff said.

Leigh glanced at him startled at the strange comment. "Day for what?"

"Old Man Brown smiling like a well-fed tabby cat. Lord, Leigh, the man is a real stickler for rules, and he's as conservative as my aunt Tilly's corset."

"You're telling me. After that first interview I thought for sure I'd be rejected. After all, I only own one-third of a building site, Leigh's Country Crafts and my plans."

"Don't forget the house on Dogwood."

"But it's not paid for, either."

"True, but it's close enough it hardly matters. Don't think that was the whole reason you got the loan."

Leigh stopped beside the car. "You're not suggest-ing—"

Jeff looked horrified at the direction of her thoughts. "No, I'm not," he denied vehemently. "What I meant was you obviously impressed him in a business way. He said as much when he returned the books to me. I believe his words were along the lines of a *damn fine head for profit and detail*.''

''I'll be darned.''

Jeff grinned, looking surprisingly young despite his forty-seven years. ''No, you'll be a success.'' With a wave, he turned and headed for his car.

Leigh stared after him, torn between shouting her jubilation from the rooftops and hugging her triumph close to her heart. For a second she wished she had someone to share her achievement with besides Sally. Someone like the tall gambler who made her world light up. But she didn't have Joshua and, in fact, he didn't know a thing about her plans. Pushing the errant wish aside, Leigh reminded herself she had chosen this way and she was happy. If a little voice inside her whispered *liar* she ignored it as she drove back to the store.

The rest of the day passed in a haze of euphoria. Sally was nearly as high as she was, making work more of a celebration than a job. By the time Leigh arrived home she was too excited to sit or eat. She couldn't ignore her need to tell Joshua any longer. She wanted to share the news with him. She even regretted the fact she had kept her plans from him. Not that she had done it consciously, yet somehow she had avoided telling him.

She couldn't help wondering how he would feel about knowing that she would now be spending part of her time in Nashville. Would he be glad? Uneasy and more than a little disturbed that it mattered to her, Leigh slumped in her chair, frowning into space. She and Joshua were lovers. She enjoyed it. He enjoyed it. They were having an affair. Neither of them were committed—

The phone rang, jerking her out of her thoughts. "Joshua," she breathed, her doubts forgotten as his voice answered hers. The husky timbre reminded her of the dark passionate nights they'd shared. For that moment he was close once more.

Nine

—

Tell me this weekend wasn't my overactive imagination."

"It wasn't your imagination," Leigh murmured, remembering the passion-filled hours vividly.

"Tell me you enjoyed it."

That was easy. "I enjoyed it."

"And you miss me."

Caught unawares at the question within the statement, Leigh hesitated then shrugged faintly. Joshua couldn't see the gesture through the phone she held, but she knew he heard the pause that preceded it.

"I miss you," she admitted. She had gone so far already. One more step wouldn't make that much difference.

Joshua's sigh of relief was clearly audible. "Woman, you had me worried," he confessed feelingly. The hesitation had been shorter than ever before, but it was still present. Complete trust was closer, but not yet his.

Leigh's brows arched. "Good! Sneaky tacticians deserve exactly what they get." Joshua's habit of slipping in questions without warning was getting easier to handle. Some she answered, like this one. Others she ignored. But at no time did she allow his strategy to go unnoticed. With him in Nashville and her safe at home, it was even simpler to handle.

"I was hoping you wouldn't catch me out this time." He paused, the light banter dropping away as though it had never been. "Could you come over sometime this week? Take the afternoon off and maybe the next morning?" He knew he was rushing her again but nothing could have stopped him from trying.

"I don't know." Staying with Joshua seemed more intimate somehow than him coming to her in Knoxville.

Joshua heard the indecision in her voice and this time rejoiced at its presence. At least she hadn't condemned the suggestion out of hand. "No strings. I promise. You can have the guest room if that's the way you want it."

Startled at the offer, Leigh was slow to reply. "Is that what you want?"

"Hell, no," Joshua all but roared. "Have I ever given you any reason to believe I'm a fool?"

The male outrage in his response tricked a chuckle out of her, which quickly turned into laughter.

"Leigh Mason, you quit giggling at me," he warned, secretly pleased at her agreement. If he'd learned anything about Leigh, it was her absolute refusal to permit a whisper of permanence, no matter how short termed, to attach itself to their relationship.

"I'm not giggling. I've never giggled in my life," Leigh protested on a gasp before one final gurgle spoiled the assertion.

Joshua ignored that in favor of the more important issue. "So when can you get here?"

"Before I answer that, there is something I want to tell you," she explained, unable to keep her news secret a moment longer.

Alerted at the sudden infusion of excitement in Leigh's usually controlled voice, Joshua probed carefully. "Tell me what?"

Leigh hesitated, realizing as she did that there was no reason for her surprise attack of cold feet. This was crazy, she assured herself. She and Joshua were lovers. She enjoyed talking to him and knew the business angle of her expansion should appeal to him. Yet she was stalling.

Annoyed with herself, she pushed her announcement out. "I'm going to be opening another Country Crafts in Nashville. I received the final bank approval today."

"Run that one by me again," Joshua murmured blankly.

"I said I'm going to be opening a store in Nashville."

"When?" The sinking in the pit of his stomach was no figment of his imagination. Had he been foolishly congratulating himself on having made headway with her in the trust department? A deal like this wasn't put through overnight. Leigh had not only known about the expansion but deliberately kept it from him. That hurt.

"By the end of summer if all goes well." Leigh frowned at his neutral replies. It was as though he were holding back some emotion.

"You've been working on this for a while."

The frown on her face deepened with puzzlement. "Yes."

"Banks usually require more than one meeting before they part with any money." Couldn't she see what she had done to him?

What was wrong? "Yes."

"I guess my offer comes at a good time for you. You would have been coming to Nashville anyway." Pain translated into anger and bitterness. He had worked so hard for so little.

Now she had a clue. Disappointment and hurt were laced in the rough cadence of his voice. "I meant to tell you but—"

Joshua interrupted. "I'm not asking for explanations."

Sighing at his attitude, Leigh clenched her fingers around the receiver. He didn't have the right to be hurt or upset. Their relationship wasn't built for it.

"You're being unrea—"

Again he cut her off. "I've got to go. I'll call you again tomorrow, and we'll set up a time that's good for us both." With the best will in the world he couldn't make his words less abrupt. If he stayed on the phone a moment longer, he would say things best left unspoken.

Before Leigh could voice a protest or her shock at his behavior, Joshua hung up. Leigh stared at the phone, her eyes wide. Anger, hurt and disbelief warred for supremacy. None won. Confusion was the order of the day as she replaced the receiver and stood up. The pleasure of her business future dimmed and that angered her more.

"He had no right," she muttered while she climbed the steps to the bedroom.

She had wanted to share her news with him!

That was a laugh. He was acting like she owed him her past and present history. No strings. No commitments. He knew the score. She had never lied to him or promised anything that she hadn't delivered. Believing he meant what he had said had been a mistake. Hadn't she learned anything with Buddy? Men were capable of all kinds of subterfuge when they wanted something badly enough.

With a sharp nod she stripped off her clothes and showered. A loose robe, a glass of chilled wine and a tray of cheese, fruit and bread relaxed her body and satisfied her physical needs. A second glass of wine even managed to dull the sharpest edges of her temper, provided she didn't think of Joshua. But nothing brought sleep an inch closer to reality as the darkness deepened with the passing hours. She was just debating the merits of an uncharacteristic third glass, over the last few swallows of the second, when the phone rang.

Leigh glanced at the sleek instrument on the table across the room knowing it was Joshua. She sipped her drink slowly while it rang twice—three times with increasing insistence. On the fifth summons she rose from her chair, put down the glass and strolled over to lift the receiver.

"Yes."

"I'm sorry. I was a fool and I know it."

"True."

Joshua inhaled sharply at the uncompromising replies. He freely acknowledged he deserved them, but he had hoped he would be wrong. "Will you be fairer than I was and let me explain?" he asked warily. He could feel her slipping away from him with every second. Cursing silently at his own stupidity, he awaited the verdict. He had promised himself he would be patient. At the first sign of freely given trust he had thrown it away because it was less than he felt he deserved. He should have been shouting for joy that she had told him at all.

Leigh started to refuse before he even finished his request. Certainly she was in no mood to be fair, to him or herself if it came to that. Yet his sincerity merited more than a flat refusal. An apology for a man like Joshua couldn't have been easy.

"All right."

Joshua shut his eyes briefly against a surge of relief. At least he had gotten this far. Now if he could just make her understand.

"I was hurt. I keep forgetting how short a time we've known each other." He had decided before he called that he'd give her total honesty. Anything less would have ruined whatever slim chance he had. Leigh's wariness was a formidable barrier, even under the best of circumstances. "There was no reason for you to tell me anything about your business."

He waited, hearing only the sounds of her breathing mingling with his in the silence that stretched across the miles separating them. Would she accept his apology? Would it be enough? Did she know that he couldn't let her go? Couldn't she feel how important she was becoming to him? Maybe she knew and needed this excuse to run. The lack of knowledge frustrated him.

"I should have told you."

Leigh's confession was so soft that Joshua almost missed it. "Why didn't you?" He risked a question.

"I could say I didn't think it was important in our relationship."

Her tone was wary, but her words invited him to probe. Feeling as though he were picking his way through a minefield, Joshua followed her lead.

"And did you tell yourself that?"

"No."

The stillness was absolute. He waited . . . hoping.

"Please, Leigh."

The plea had the power no demand could have ever had. Sighing, she gave him one more clue to her personality, one more sliver of solitude was shared to become part of a pairing.

"Country Crafts is mine. I planned, financed it and worried over it. It was there when I needed something to hang on to. I've forgotten how to share."

Joshua swallowed the lump her painful words brought to his throat. She was so alone. She had courage and strength in abundance but she also had the fear of a small, damaged creature, half-wild, ready to fight to the last breath if attacked but equally prepared to stay hidden in some friendly thicket and remain unseen forever.

"You haven't completely, you know," he disagreed huskily while privately blessing the physical distance between them. If they had been in the same room he knew he would never have been able to resist gathering her in his arms. That he couldn't do until she relaxed with him once more and he regained every inch of ground his stupidity had cost him.

"That's different," she denied finally, misunderstanding him completely.

Knowing it was time to ease the strain of the conversation, he laughed softly at the prim tone. "*That* wasn't what I meant, although you can add it to the list any time you want."

Intrigued at what he did mean, Leigh lay back on the bed. "Well..." she prompted when no further explanation was forthcoming.

"Has it occurred to you a loner would never spend as much time with me on the phone just talking? Do you realize neither of us do more than come up for air before we turn blue from lack of oxygen?"

Leigh chuckled at the accurate picture he drew. "We are terrible, aren't we?" she agreed, snuggling into the pillows. The lights were too bright, she decided with an inward sigh. Reaching across the bed, she flipped them off.

"Beyond redemption." Joshua propped his feet on his desk. "Now tell me all about this project of yours. Every tiny detail and don't gloat. It's not nice."

The velvety darkness of the bedroom wrapped around her body as Joshua's slow drawl soothed her into contentment. The excitement of her accomplishment softened into a deep glow of achievement. Suddenly it was easy to share the doubts, hopes and seemingly endless effort needed to bring her vision alive. Joshua's interest was real, his questions astute and his admiration all she could have hoped for. When they finally said goodbye, it was reluctantly given and received. The lingering silence between the last word and the click of the phone returning to its resting place was long.

Leigh lifted her hand away from the receiver, aware of delicious weariness drawing her deeper into the covers. It was arranged. She would leave Knoxville early Thursday and drive back from Nashville the following Monday. She and Joshua would have four nights and three days together, and she would have a day and a half to take care of business. Smiling in the

darkness, she drifted off to sleep, well content with her
life once more.

Leigh expertly switched to the far right lane in
preparation for leaving the interstate. Nashville was
sprawled around her. The vivid green of the spring-
dressed countryside touched gently against steel-and-
concrete structures creating Music City, U.S.A. Bill-
boards proclaiming All Roads Lead to Nashville
seemed to pop up like huge square mushrooms, at-
testing to the city's proud belief in itself. Traffic was
heavy due to the usual influx of visitors for this time
of the year. Leigh smiled in pleasure as she passed
buses of tourists being conducted about the town. Although she had researched the new location thoroughly, it was nice to see visible proof of the wisdom
of her choice.

Following Joshua's directions, Leigh found his office without getting lost. Fortunately there was an
empty slot in the parking lot adjacent to the building
that housed Dancer Investments. She left the car to
stare at the glass-and-metal structure, grateful she was
wearing her sunglasses against the glare. The complex
shone with reflected brilliance in the midday sun, but
the lobby was cool and dim. Hesitating momentarily,
she allowed her eyes to adjust to the change before she
crossed to the elevators.

A few minutes later she got her first glimpse of
Joshua's business in operation. Walking through the
plain, discreetly-lettered door, she felt as if she had
entered a strange world. Subdued lighting and sleek,

modernistic furniture blended with emerald carpeting, cream walls and wide glass expanses framing a panoramic view of Nashville's skyline.

"May I help you?"

Leigh focused on the slight, elegantly dressed woman in front of her. "Ms. Mason for Mr. Dancer," she said, her voice calm. The cool professionalism of the receptionist was a skillful blend of deference and impersonal courtesy that Leigh admired. The woman's attitude fit in well with her surroundings. What was surprising and unexpected was the friendly smile her name generated in the brunette.

"I'm supposed to send you right in but a client dropped by unexpectedly to see Joshua. She's with him now."

Leigh's brow arched slightly at the apology in her tone. "That's all right. I'll wait," she replied, wondering at the change.

The receptionist rose. "Could I get you some coffee? Or juice if you prefer?" She grinned suddenly, her pale eyes twinkling. "I guess I should introduce myself too. I'm Jilly Baker."

Leigh took a seat, completely at sea. What on earth had Joshua told Jilly? "Coffee will be fine. Black." Leigh watched the woman disappear down the hall only to reappear, cup in hand, a moment later.

"Here you are." Jilly took a chair across from Leigh. "Did you have a nice trip?"

Leigh sipped the brew gingerly before she answered. "Yes, I made good time." She'd never felt more awkward in her life. Darn Joshua for getting her into this.

Jilly nodded. "I heard about what you did for Missy. That was really brave. I guess a few hundred miles is easy compared to something like that."

Startled that a stranger would know so much about her, Leigh waited with carefully concealed impatience for a clue as to who Jilly was. The creature was clearly more than "just" the receptionist. In fact, she was also at least ten years older than the twenty-five or six Leigh had first guessed her to be.

"I was hoping you'd be nice. Joshua's such a super person. He deserves someone special."

That did it. Leigh's head came up, her eyes growing cold with annoyance that Joshua would discuss her with someone she didn't know. "You have the advantage of me." What right had Joshua to tell this woman anything? "You obviously know about me but—" She allowed her voice to trail off meaningfully.

Jilly stared at her, her expression changing from friendly to surprise then to amusement in a second. She laughed softly, the husky sound strangely reminiscent of Joshua. "I thought you knew. I'm Joshua's first cousin. We grew up together."

"Cousin?" Leigh had thought Joshua had no other family beyond his stepsister.

"And personal secretary, except for today. I'm playing greeting lady since our regular woman's sick. The rest of the staff are at lunch. Joshua was waiting for you when 'Disgraceful Dédé' showed up."

Leigh choked on her coffee at the droll nickname and the wicked smile that accompanied it.

"Well, she is," Jilly mumbled, casting a wary eye down the hall. "Not that I'd say this to anyone else but you and Joshua."

"Why me?" Leigh demanded in a faint croak. "You don't know me from Adam's house cat."

Jilly grinned. "No, but Joshua does and *he's* been bending my ear about you since he came back from Knoxville three weeks ago. I can't wait until you open a store here. Joshua says the one in Knoxville is fantastic. I know he's over the moon at the prospect of Missy putting her talents to use for you." She studied Leigh with surprisingly shrewd eyes. "And now I've convinced you I tell everything I know to anyone who comes down the road, haven't I?"

Leigh couldn't help it, she had to laugh. Jilly's expression was anything but sincere. Dark brows over vivid green eyes rose in devilish arcs. She had the Dancer charm, their wicked sense of humor and, Leigh suspected, the same code of honor.

"Truly?" Leigh echoed teasingly, doing a little sparring of her own. "I never would have believed it with this performance."

"It was rather good, wasn't it."

"Passable, not inspired."

"It caught you flat-footed a couple of times."

"For a second, maybe," Leigh agreed honestly, privately vowing to have a word with her silver-tongued lover about the inadvisability of being so free with his compliments and confidences. She wasn't accustomed to life in the Dancer fishbowl, pleasant though the company seemed to be.

The sound of the door opening and voices drew both women's attention to the room at the end of the hall. The tall, voluptuous form in skin-tight leather pants, wild print shirt drawn snug over luscious curves raised Jilly's brows. Leigh was fine until scarlet-tipped nails tapped Joshua's lean cheek far too familiarly. Her blood pressure gave a leap that caught her by surprise.

"The woman's a she-wolf," Jilly muttered, through lips stretched into a professional smile that neither of the pair saw.

Leigh watched the secretary get to her feet while she sought to grab her temper with both hands. She-shark was more like it, Leigh decided, staring at the over blown body pressed against Joshua's side. Neither Joshua nor the Disgraceful Dédé was aware of their audience as far as Leigh could tell. What the devil was he doing letting her paw him like that, Leigh fumed.

"Another half-inch and she'll be wearing Joshua's clothes," Leigh breathed, forgetting Jilly was close enough to hear.

Jilly choked on a laugh, drawing the duo's attention. Judging from her expression, Dédé was distinctly displeased at the interruption. Joshua, on the other hand, looked like a man escaping from *Jaws* with all of his limbs intact.

"Leigh, I had no idea you were here," he said, coming toward her, his hands outstretched.

Leigh rose to catch his fingers in hers without a second thought. An instant later she was pulled into an embrace guaranteed to discourage Dédé and blow her own composure out of orbit.

"Joshua," she murmured when he released her, "that's some welcome."

He grinned at her, his dark eyes alight with mischief and lambent desire. "It has been four days." Turning, he introduced Leigh to the now silent Dédé. There was no doubt the singer had gotten the message. The fact was plainly evident in her speedy departure.

"I didn't know you had it in you."

"Be quiet, Jilly," Joshua commanded while leveling a warning look at his talkative relative. "That was a survival skill in action."

Jilly snorted, glancing at Leigh. "Are you going to let him get away with that?"

"No, but I am waiting to retaliate until we're without an audience."

Joshua stared at her, arrested by the not so calm look on Leigh's face. "You are?"

"Oh ho, the worm has turned," Jilly chortled gleefully. "The minute I saw her I knew she was woman enough to stand up to you."

"Go type a letter or something," Joshua ordered, his eyes never leaving Leigh. "What form will this revenge take?" he asked. He couldn't believe it. That was jealousy blazing out of her eyes.

Leigh allowed her gaze to sweep him from head to toe and back again before answering. "What form would you like it to take?'' No strings and no commitments didn't mean she couldn't lay down a rule or two. The first one being one man, one woman.

"A kiss?" he inquired hopefully.

"Not enough." He'd remember what they had, temporary though it was, or she would know the reason why.

"A kiss and a hug?"

"Try again."

"A kiss, a hug and a cuddle?" That gleam in her eyes was definitely unnerving.

Standing on tiptoe, Leigh brushed his ear with her lips. "How about a kiss, a hug, and—" By the time she leaned away from Joshua's body, red had surged under his skin, drawing an amazed look from Jilly.

Leigh smiled provocatively. "Ready, lover?" Tucking her hand in his, she headed for the door with Joshua following docilely. "He may not be back for the rest of the day," she added, glancing over her shoulder.

The sight of Jilly's dumbfounded expression was a sweet return and made up for the first meeting with the outspoken Dancer cousin. In one stroke she had floored two of the clan, and she intended to savor every minute of her victory. One satisfying aspect of being a lover was that she could indulge in tactics a girlfriend or wife might balk at. The fact that she felt the need to establish her rights unsettled her a little, but not nearly as much as the sight of Dédé draped around Joshua like a sexy snake.

Ten

***

I like your house,'' Leigh said, turning away from the window.

She and Joshua were in the living room, the first and only room she'd seen. Leigh's remark was the result of an exterior view of the secluded home and the rich elegance of the interior now surrounding her. Joshua made no comment as he stood a few feet away, hands jammed in his pockets watching her. Architecture was the last thing on his mind at the moment. He was still trying to come to terms with the scenario Leigh had whispered in his ear. The thought had his blood simmering and it was all he could do to keep his hands to himself.

"The lake is beautiful. It's so peaceful here it's hard to believe there are other houses around."

"Is it?" he murmured absently. She looked so right standing there. Just as if she belonged in his home among his favorite things.

Leigh hid a smile at his vague reply. He was still unnerved by her ploy at the office. She would have expected him to recover quickly. Surely, she hadn't been the first woman to proposition him.

"Earth to Joshua."

Joshua blinked, really focusing on her for the first time since she'd whispered her outrageous suggestion in his ear. Before he knew it, he was voicing the questions swirling in his mind.

"Brandy? Peaches? A fire? Do you have any idea what your little scenario did to me? And in front of Jilly?" He raked his fingers through his hair, torn between shaking her and dragging her into the den where he just happened to have every item of her risqué fantasy except the peaches. The thought of making her suggestion a reality boggled his mind and played havoc with his libido.

Hearing the stunned disbelief in his tone, Leigh frowned, momentarily assailed by doubts. It hadn't occurred to her he might not like her taking the initiative. "The idea doesn't appeal?" she asked carefully.

"Appeal? I'd be crazy if it didn't," he shot back, stalking toward her. He caught her shoulders then forced himself to be more gentle. His arousal demanded action. Restraining himself was an exercise in self-denial. Leigh was not a woman for roughness, no matter what the provocation.

"Right now you look as innocent as the day you were born. Twenty minutes ago you would have made a courtesan seem like a nun."

Leigh tilted her head back, her lashes half closing against the relief flowing through her. It was all right after all. She hadn't disgusted or shocked him.

"Woman, you've got more turns than a crooked road."

"A courtesan? And now a crooked road. I love your compliments."

"And I love the feel of you in my arms. Your skin is as soft as a tabby's pelt. Your mouth is sweeter than my best wine."

"More compliments?"

Swinging her in his arms, Joshua strode to the door. "No, I'm just getting you in the mood for a certain date with a fireplace and a glass of brandy...."

Leigh cuddled against him, content to let him carry her. It was something no one but him had ever done before. "At one o'clock in the afternoon?" she teased as she inhaled the male scent of his warm body. Had man always smelled this good? Or was it just Joshua?

"And probably again at two, three and four."

"Superman."

Joshua kicked open the study door, which was only slightly ajar. "Desperate and it's all your fault."

Leigh had a vague impression of books, oak paneling and a rich amber decor. The fireplace faced a floor-to-ceiling bank of windows. The view was sen-

sational if Leigh had been interested. She wasn't. She
only had eyes for Joshua as he lowered her to her feet,
his body imprinting itself on her soft curves with familiar ease.

"I never meant to make you desperate."

"I know. You were only trying to get a little of your
own back." Framing her face with his palms, he gazed
into the clear, bottomless depths of her eyes. "I'm
glad you came. I wasn't sure you would."

"I'm glad I came too. I wanted to be with you."

"And your fantasy?"

"A reality if you wish."

Joshua groaned before taking her lips with undis-
guised hunger. "Do you need to ask?" he gasped
when he raised his head to breathe.

"No," she whispered, sinking down on the soft rug
on which they stood.

Joshua was right beside her all the way. The hearth
was empty of a flame, but a bonfire raged as two became one in a swift joining where words were a waste
of precious seconds and far too shallow to convey the
desire they shared. It was over too soon, leaving them
in a tangle of damp limbs, their breaths mingling while
they lay side by side.

"I'll never move again."

Joshua chuckled softly, lightly stroking her hair
away from her face. "Yes, you will. I promise."

Leigh smiled at him, aware of a deep contentment
turning her bones to warm taffy. "We aren't going to
try for a two o'clock romp, are we?"

"Romp? Watch your tongue, lady. Besides, why not? We did your fantasy."

"We did not. There's no fire in the fireplace. I never got my brandy or the first glimpse of a peach."

Joshua ran his hand gently over her body from breast to thigh. "Are you complaining?" he asked before he dipped his head to lightly nibble at the peak quivering expectantly for his touch.

Leigh inhaled softly at the slow, delicious lovemaking. The weight of his hand lying just at the gateway of her femininity was a sweet torment that fanned the flame of desire. "Joshua," she gasped when he saluted the second pink-tipped crest.

"Leigh," he echoed while he fit himself against her. "The books say this isn't possible."

"Prove them wrong," she demanded, wrapping her arms and legs around him in erotic invitation.

Joshua needed no second command. He took her then slowly, savoring every inch of possession, delighting in the feel of her responsive body beneath his. If the first mating had been white-hot, this one was a leisurely slide into oblivion. Sleep crept softly over them at the end of the long journey, wrapping a blanket of peace around satiated bodies and passion-drugged minds.

"What are your plans while I'm at work today?" Joshua asked. He glanced up when Leigh placed a plate in front of him.

Leigh deposited a similarly laden platter of scrambled eggs, bacon and toast before her own chair then sat down. "I have an appointment with the contractor and the architect this morning. Then I'll meet you for lunch if you have time. After that I have a couple of errands to run for the store."

Joshua frowned. "Is that going to give you enough time to get ready for the party tonight?"

Leigh looked at him, surprised at the question. "Why shouldn't it? I thought I might even treat myself to a shopping trip for a new dress."

"I don't want you rushing around just for me. Tonight's not that important."

"You're serious," she breathed in amazement. When Joshua had first told her about the gathering he'd been invited to, he'd explained it was more a business appearance than a social occasion. He had also been anything but pleased at the intrusion in their weekend.

"I understood you to say this was a potential major client."

Joshua shrugged. "He is but it's still not worth running yourself ragged. If Willy Joe wants Dancer Investments to handle his affairs, then he'll have to make up his mind without my appearance at this bash." Picking up his fork, he resumed eating. The subject was closed. "These eggs are good. What's in them?"

"Swiss cheese, mushrooms and a little onion," she replied automatically while trying to comprehend how easily he had altered his plans to suit her.

First, it had been the dinner last night that he'd insisted on cooking since she had driven most of yesterday morning. Then there had been the sharing of chores after they had gotten up today. With the maid off, there had been a bed to make—he'd done that— dirty clothes and towels to take down to the laundry room—also his job. She had tackled breakfast while he had been busy upstairs.

Leigh tried to think if Buddy had ever shared the housework. Her answer had to be a resounding no. He hadn't minded her working, but he had expected his home to be perfect, ready for them to entertain at a moment's notice. He hadn't lifted a finger to help out, nor had he ever put her pleasure before the demands of the career he'd been carving out for himself.

"Thank you."

Joshua glanced up at the quiet words, his gaze holding her solemn one. One brow crooked upward as he asked, "For what?"

Leigh almost said for being you but stopped herself just in time. It was too easy to let Joshua deeper into her life. He slipped through her defenses and touched raw places she had thought hidden. She wanted to pull away, yet it was impossible. Telling herself that it was his lovemaking that held her in thrall was becoming more difficult by the day.

"I like an understanding man," she said instead, trying for a light note.

Just for a moment he had been sure she would say something quite different, something important. Instead, she had retreated yet again. He was beginning to believe she would never come any closer than she was now. A second later he remembered he hadn't expected her to come this far. Maybe there was still hope.

"I try." There were so many things he wanted to say. He swallowed every one of them. They would only push her away. He pointed to her plate. "Finish your eggs. You've got a full day ahead of you."

"Bossy."

"Probably. I've been dealing with Missy too long."

"You would make a good father." Leigh almost dropped her fork, realizing what she had said. How could she have been so stupid?

Joshua lifted his head to stare at her. It was the first time she had ever mentioned being a parent except in regard to Missy. "I like to think so," he said slowly, wondering what had drained her face of color. Her hands were in her lap and at a guess he would say they were twisting with nerves even though her expression was calm. Suddenly he knew that the time had come to take a chance. To probe for the rest of her past, the part that still had the power to hurt her and make her stiffen in his arms.

"What about you? Would you like children?"

Leigh paled even more. For one moment she almost took the coward's way out. She had evaded him before. She could do it again. Her lashes closed as she tried to make a choice. Some part of her recognized she had brought this discussion about. An unconscious wish, perhaps, to cleanse her conscience.

"I can't have children," she said without opening her eyes. She couldn't bear to see the pity on his face when she told him. He might not love her, but he did care for her.

Silence, long and deep, filled the room. Leigh could not have moved if her life depended on it. She couldn't look at him, either. The sound of his chair scraping the floor made her flinch but not nearly as much as the hands that caught her shoulders and pulled her to her feet.

"Look at me, Leigh," Joshua commanded. "What do you mean you can't have children?"

Slowly, Leigh opened her eyes. "Just that," she whispered, tears starting at the pain of the wound that had never healed. "The doctors had to take more than just my baby to save my life."

Joshua stared at her, seeing all the pain and finally understanding the depth of destruction that her past held. "That's why he left, isn't it?" The horrifying knowledge was like a knife in his gut. That a man could leave a woman like Leigh, after a blow of this magnitude, was beyond his comprehension.

"Wouldn't you have?" Leigh shrugged out of his hold. "I was no good to him any more. That's why I don't want commitments. I don't have anything a man would want."

Stunned, Joshua was slow to react. That a woman of Leigh's obvious intelligence could believe such drivel was beyond his comprehension. "You can't think that. What the devil does it matter to a man who loves you? There is always adoption. There are hundreds of children who need homes in this world."

Leigh swung around, angry that he could not see the truth. "It's not the same," she all but shouted. "Don't you think I thought of that. I even suggested it to Buddy. Do you know what he did? He smiled at me as if I were a backward toddler. It's not the same for a man, honey, he said. And there was pity in his eyes that I was too stupid not to realize the truth."

"No, damn it, it isn't the same. But only that insensitive clod would be so cruel as to tell you that when you were lying in a hospital, still in shock from the accident." Josh caught her shoulders, hurting for her and with her. "You're well now. It's time you started thinking clearly, seeing your ex for what he was and seeing yourself as more than a baby-making machine."

"You sound like my doctor. He tried to tell him the same platitudes when he was explaining what he had done to me." Leigh stared at Joshua without really seeing him. Instead she looked into the past, remembering that black day. "He held my hand as he sat beside my bed. His voice was so kind as he carefully gave me all the medical wording of what had happened to my baby and to me. 'I had to take the ovary. There was no way to stop the bleeding otherwise.'" She blinked, focusing on Josh's face once more. "He saved my life, he said." She laughed harshly. "I don't know why he bothered. I haven't felt alive since."

"Leigh, don't—" Josh stopped as the words she had just said suddenly penetrated. "Tell me exactly what the doctor said again, Leigh. Now!" he commanded in an altered tone.

Shocked out of her pain at the strength of his grip on her shoulders and the urgent note in his voice she obeyed. "That he had cut out the ovary. That it had ruptured and I was bleeding internally."

"He didn't say two? Are you sure?"

Leigh stared at him, frowning at the question. "Two what?"

"Two ovaries. A woman has two ovaries, Leigh. Not one. You know that." Josh was almost afraid to hope. But if Leigh remembered correctly, then she was not barren as she believed. "Surely he explained more clearly at some point in time. I can't believe you didn't ask questions."

Leigh pulled at his hands, unable to deal with what he was saying. Her head swung from side to side and she didn't even realize it. "What good would questions have done? I lay there in that bed and he told me all that he had done. I couldn't face any more, not after Buddy came in and said he would not be there when I got out of the hospital. That he needed to get away. I lay there for two weeks before I was discharged. I counted the seconds until I could leave. I promised myself no doctor would ever get a chance to take part of me away again. No man would ever sign a stupid piece of paper when I was unconscious and couldn't decide for myself what my life was worth."

Leigh inhaled deeply, barely hanging on to her sanity as the words poured out of her. "The day I walked out of that hospital is the day I started packing. One week later, the morning I was to see that man who had left me empty was the last time I saw Chicago."

Josh froze. "You never saw the doctor?"

"No!"

"My god, Leigh! All this time you have been torturing yourself over something that may not even be true. Don't you realize it? Can't you see?"

Leigh backed away. "You're lying. You're just like Buddy. If I can't have children, then I'm no good."

Joshua moved then, too angry to let her tear at him that way. "That's not true. I'd want you if you were in a wheelchair and I had to feed you every day for the rest of your life." He caught her as she tried to run, swinging her into his arms. He wasn't going to allow her to withdraw from him now. He had worked too long and too hard to gain her trust. She would not destroy it. He would prove to her that he was not like Buddy.

Leigh was past controlling her emotions. Her fists beat at his chest in a frenzy of pain and frustration. "I don't believe you," she wept.

"I know," he growled above her head, ignoring her blows if he even felt them. All his attention was on the stairs he climbed to the bedroom they had shared. He placed her in the bed and followed her down before she could slide away.

"I won't let you make love to me," she panted as she struggled to evade his hands.

Joshua ignored her, stripping her as efficiently as he had the night before. "You will, you know. And when we're done you'll know I'm telling you the truth." He rolled over her, pinning her to the bed. "Neither of us can hide when we are like this. There are no secrets here. Listen to your heart. Hear mine.''

With that he bent his head and began a lesson in trust and truth that Leigh would never forget. He gave. He took. He cried with her and for her. He filled the emptiness with life and burned the coldness from her body with the fires of his own passion. When it was over, his eyes looked into hers and there was no room for lies, evasions or hesitations.

"You cannot change what happened here this morning,'' Josh said quietly, watching her. "You are mine. I am yours. We will face your past. Whatever it is.''

"I'm afraid,'' she confessed, feeling him in every bone and sinew. His taste was in her mouth, his hands held her securely in the curve of his warmth. And still she feared.

"I'll be there. I promise.''

Her eyes searched his. He was offering her all that she had thought lost. Was she brave enough to take a chance? "Does it have to be now? I need time,'' she pleaded finally.

Joshua wanted to refuse. Every nerve in him said that she should find out the truth at once. Yet he could not make himself force her. She had lived with the destruction for so long, perhaps she did need time to adjust, to believe that a future might be possible.

"All right. Take your time but don't shut me out. I'm here, and here is where I'm staying no matter what you do.''

* * *

As if those words were some kind of pact signed by
both, their life fell into a pattern over the next month.
Joshua came to Knoxville on alternate weekends,
leaving a few clothes and personal items at her house.
Leigh, in turn, spent at least one workday plus Saturday and Sunday in Nashville with Joshua. It hardly
seemed worth the trouble to carry a case back and
forth, so some of her clothes took up residence in the
master-bedroom closet. Leigh recognized they had
virtually moved in together, but she said nothing aloud
and neither did Joshua. Nor did they discuss her past.
Joshua had clearly taken her at her word and given her
the time and space she needed to come to grips with
the possibility that she might not be barren. If Leigh
found him watching her a little more closely than
usual, she ignored the look. If she couldn't do that she
teased him out of his serious mood. All the while she
wrestled with the dark demons of the past and the
shadows of Buddy's desertion. That is, the sane, rational part of her knew Joshua wasn't Buddy. She
couldn't believe, perhaps was afraid to believe, that
this happiness that lay in the palm of her hand would
last whether she was barren or not. So she waited,
hoping, fearing and loving in spite of herself.

Then Joshua dropped his bombshell.

"You want to do what?" Leigh exclaimed.

Leigh stared at him as if he had suddenly sprouted
horns. Pushing herself out of his arms, she half fell,
half rolled out of bed.

Joshua watched her scramble off the mattress and snatch on a light robe. Eyes narrowing at her unexpected reaction, he made no immediate attempt to answer her. Instead he asked a question of his own.

"What are you afraid of? Haven't these last weeks shown you we can live together and love together? Don't you trust me completely even yet?"

Taking a restless step away, Leigh whirled around, the robe swirling out to reveal long legs stiff with tension. "Of course I trust you. Do you think I would be here if I did not?" She could have cried at the way she described their lovemaking and the emotions he created within her. Still she plunged on, waving a hand at the bed. "What's wrong with the relationship we have now? It works. I enjoy it. I'd be a liar if I said I didn't. But marriage?" She shook her head, wishing she dared accept his offer. But she couldn't bear it if they wed and he turned away from her later. Better this than nothing. "I can't do it. You know why."

Joshua shot out of bed, stung by the adamantly dismissing tone in her voice. "No, I don't know why," he all but shouted, angry and hurt at her attitude. "Haven't you learned anything these past few weeks? I want a life with you, with or without children, and I won't let you throw that away because of some insane fear that may not even be true. What we have is too important, too special. You're more woman than I've ever known. I want to grow old with you beside me. I don't have any immediate family but Missy, and she's making her own life now. You're alone, too. Do you want to spend the rest of your life like this?" He caught her shoulders, staring into her suddenly pale face. "I want to be more than your lover and your friend. I want to be your husband, too."

"Well, I don't want to be your wife," she shot back.

Joshua took her in his arms. "Don't you, Leigh?" he asked, his eyes daring her to lie.

Leigh opened her lips to do just that and found she couldn't. Tears welled in pools to finally overflow down her cheeks in silent streams. The pain on his face was more than she could take. She had to give him the truth. "I do want to be your wife. I want to have your children. I can't tell you how much. But I can't make myself go back. Don't you understand? I'm afraid to find out the truth. I'm afraid to hear those words again. I think of it every day when I wake up. It's with me when I go to sleep. And still I can't get up the nerve to make a call. To find out for sure."

Joshua gathered her close, absorbing her tremors with his body. "Why didn't you tell me, love? I would have saved you all of this."

Leigh pressed her face against his chest, hardly hearing his words. "I'm so ashamed. It should be so easy."

"Why?" he demanded. "You lived this way for five years. It almost tore your heart out the first time to learn what you believed to be the truth. Only fools put themselves deliberately in the path of pain. And you are no fool. No matter how this comes out you will be hurt. Hurt that you wasted five years living a lie or that it is true and there is no hope." He tipped her head back so that she had to look at him. "I understand. But more than that I love you."

Leigh stared at him, reading the truth in his eyes. She should have known. The understanding and the love had been why she had kept coming back to Nashville and accepting his presence in her home when she had accepted no one else. She hadn't wanted to admit that either love or understanding existed. For to acknowledge them would be a demand for more than she felt she had to give. It still was. His love meant that she had to be stronger than she believed possible, and that she had to face the past and find out the truth. That she had to take a chance that if she was barren Joshua would still love her and want to marry her. What if he did stay by her side while she got her answers but once found, discovered that he did not want her. That was the worse fear of all. Could she survive going through that again?

"I want to book us a flight to Chicago. We'll see that doctor and hear what he has to say together." Joshua's voice was quiet but determined.

Leigh knew she couldn't put it off any longer. She had to make a choice. Taking her courage in her hands, she took the risk. "All right."

Her reward was a smile that held more admiration than joy, more relief than triumph. "Today?"

She could manage no more than a nod.

Joshua kissed her then, hard, quickly and thoroughly before letting her go. "We won't stay unless you want to."

"No. I would rather come straight back home," she replied quietly.

"Home it is." Never had one four-lettered word sounded so good to him. Never had he saluted Leigh's courage more. Never had he prayed for anything as hard as he did for the mistake he believed had been made. Not for himself, but for her.

Eleven

—

It's done,'' Joshua announced from behind Leigh. He slipped his arms around her waist and pulled her against him. "We leave in the morning for Chicago. The flight's not long. We will arrive in time to be the first appointment with the doctor. The return trip is at one in the afternoon.''

He waited, hoping she would say something, anything. Since Leigh had agreed to the trip she had been impossibly quiet. She'd refused to stay with him while he made the arrangements, preferring to go to the kitchen and make coffee. He could understand her apprehension, but he could not help feeling shut out because she would not talk to him.

Leigh leaned against Joshua, absorbing his strength. She had not lied when she admitted she was scared. For so long she had believed she could not have children. Her whole life was based on the premise. Now in one stroke all that could be changed. It was so much to take in. What if it had not been a misunderstanding? What if the hope she was beginning to feel wasn't the truth?

Suddenly she could not stand the questions any more. She turned and looped her arms around his neck. "I need you," she said breathlessly, risking rejection for the first time since Buddy had deserted her. "Make love to me."

Joshua read the desperation in her eyes as clearly as if she had shouted it. A shaft of pain slipped under his ribs. He could have been anyone at that moment, he swore silently. It was oblivion she sought, not him.

Gathering her closer, he gave her the solace she asked for. He loved her too much to refuse. "For as long as you like, love," he whispered, taking her lips as he lifted her body against his chest.

The bedroom was too far so he took her to the den. There on the shag rug before the fire Joshua wove a web of forgetfulness. Leigh lost the past, the pain and the fear in his passion. When it was over, she slept in his arms, neither knowing nor caring that the day had begun. When she awoke he was there. His eyes looked into hers, seeing her as no one else had ever done.

"I'm sorry," she whispered.

Joshua searched her face. "For what?"

"Using you. That was cruel."

He nodded slightly. "It was. But it was also beautiful. We make magic love together."

Leigh could not let him forgive her so easily. "But it wasn't fair to you," she persisted.

Joshua smiled gently. "If this is the most unfair thing you ever do after we're married, I'll take it."

"I haven't said yes," she reminded him, stiffening.

Joshua felt the withdrawal instantly. His hand stroked down her bare body from breast to thigh, easing the tension from the slender limbs. "No, you haven't but you will. Because you see I know something you don't. I won't leave you. I won't run if you are barren, and I won't let you drive me away with your insecurities if you aren't. I meant what I said. I'll take you with or without children. And nothing you can say will change that."

Leigh wanted to believe, desperately. "You're so sure."

"I am. I love you. That won't change." He shook her once, lovingly. "But I do have a question for you." He would keep her mind off the next day if he had to run her ragged to do it. He would not allow her time to brood if they had to make love for every second of the hours that remained until they boarded the plane.

Leigh softened against him at the firm reassurance. For now she would let herself believe. She needed his strength. If he did nothing else but help her through the doctor's visit....

"Leigh, stop thinking," Joshua commanded, seeing that stoic acceptance he so disliked settling over her face. "Answer my question."

Blinking, Leigh focused on his face. "What is it?"

"How would you like to go on a picnic?"

"Now? You're crazy. I'm not in a picnic mood."

"Okay, then we'll stay here and make love all afternoon." He glanced around as though assessing the room for exotic possibilities. "After I go out for peaches, that is."

Leigh caught his arms, her fingers clamping around the hard muscles. "I'm not in the mood for using you again, either," she retorted, half-angrily.

He looked down at her, brows raised over challenging eyes. "Then what are you in the mood for, lady mine? Worrying? Sitting in a corner and killing yourself by inches trying to make your life work?" He smiled then, and this time there was no gentleness in the gesture. It was pure dare, a gambler's gauntlet thrown down on the field of honor.

Leigh frowned, not liking the wording at all. But she also could not deny that essentially Joshua was right. That had been exactly what she would have done if she had been alone.

"What kind of picnic?" she asked finally.

He hugged her, pressing a kiss to her lips. One forefinger smoothed the lines from her brow. "The kind with champagne, strawberries, pâté and cheese. The kind with no ants, no rain and, best of all, no rocks in inconvenient places under the blanket."

Intrigued despite herself, Leigh smiled and replied, "I've never been to one of those."

Joshua got to his feet, pulling her up with him. He gave Leigh a grin that no one but a blind fool would describe as anything but wicked. "Then you haven't lived." He picked up her clothes and tossed them to her. "Get dressed and I'll show you how it is done."

The how was fun, Leigh discovered. One phone call to a very expensive French restaurant produced the elegant food. A hall closet produced a soft plaid blanket that had probably never seen a rock in its short life, and the garage contributed a restored Mustang convertible Leigh had never seen. Tennessee herself did its part with an idyllic river bank complete with lacy willows and white ducks swimming beside the shore. The sun shone as though it too wished to get into the act. For a few magic hours Leigh forgot the past and the future. All that existed was this moment and the man who loved her.

But even elegant pastimes have an end. Night came and so did the tension. Still Joshua was there; he held her when she couldn't sleep, saying nothing, demanding nothing—he simply gave. In the morning he was still there through the short breakfast she couldn't eat and through the seemingly interminable plane ride carrying her back into the past. Leigh looked over the Chicago streets as the cab took them into town seeing nothing, feeling less. The closer they got to their destination the more numb she felt. She didn't even react when the receptionist called their name, nor when the doctor said the words they had come to hear. She held Joshua's hand and concentrated on holding it. He was the only stable thing in her world, the only rock she could cling to.

Joshua watched Leigh close down within herself, worried at the change but helpless to stop it. He thought she would react at the doctor's but she had not. She had simply sat there, those blank eyes staring at the man who held the key to her future. He wanted to shelter her in his arms then, but had not dared. Instead he held on to the one contact she seemed to demand, the linking of their hands. Her fingers were so tight around his that he could feel the pain of her grip. He welcomed that pain, needed it because it meant that on some level Leigh wanted him. Only an "I love you" from her lips could have meant more to him at that moment.

So he held on, guiding her through the interview, hearing the words they had come to hear with only one portion of his mind. The outcome of the visit had never been as important to him as it was to Leigh. He had meant what he said.

The return to Nashville was as silent as the trip to Chicago had been. Leigh sat beside him hardly moving as he drove back to his house. Shock, the doctor had told him. It would wear off soon. Then she would talk, share her feelings. But would she? Despite his assurances to her the day before, he wasn't all that certain they did have a future together. Leigh had never said yes to his proposal. She had never said she loved him, either. She was still Solitaire, still facing her demons alone, still shutting him out. Only the fact that she hadn't withdrawn completely gave him any hope at all, and even that was stretched tissue thin.

When they returned home Joshua shut the front door, then tugged Leigh down the hall to the study. He sat down in the huge overstuffed chair by the fire and pulled her into his lap. Taking her face in his hands, he stared into her eyes, waiting for the life to flow back into the emotionless depths. "Leigh, talk to me. Let me help."

Leigh did not react at first. Then slowly he watched her focus. She blinked once, her tears welling. Her fingers came up to trace his mouth. The tears slipped down her pale cheeks to fall onto his suit vest. They would leave a stain but neither noticed.

His own eyes misted. He read it all too well because he loved her that much. "Don't love. Don't grieve," he pleaded, drawing her close. "Let it go."

As if his words were the primer for the pump of feelings, Leigh spoke. "All these years. I believed it all these years. Day after day I woke up and wished I had died so that at least one child of my body had lived. I looked at babies and felt so empty, useless. I drove myself to blot out the past. I hid away so no one would know my secret." She laughed brokenly. "And it was all a lie. You were right about so many things. So right." Her voice cracked and then she was crying, her mouth open, her face pressed against Joshua's chest.

Tears flowed down his cheeks, christening the bright fall of her hair with his own grief and joy. Leigh could have the children that were so important to her. Only one ovary had been removed. It would be more difficult for her to get pregnant but not impossible. The doctor's words rang in his ears. Just let it be my children she wants, he prayed as he held her. Let it be me she needs now that she is free from the past.

Leigh wept for all that she had thought lost, and discovered had been hers all along. She wept too for the woman that had been destroyed by her husband's desertion. She wept for the one who had built a barren life to match her barren body. She cried for the future she would not have had but for Joshua. Holding onto him, she poured out every emotion she had. When it was done she should have felt empty. She raised her head and saw his rakish, I'll dare the devil, face. Black eyes, as deep as the heart of the night, looked into her soul with an uncertainty she had never seen before.

Love, pure as the first instant of sunrise, glistened in her heart. She wasn't empty at all. She was filled to overflowing. Filled with him. With Joshua.

"I...love...you." The words came out slowly, deliberately. Every letter separate. Every word crisp, new.

It was his turn to be really afraid. "It's not gratitude?" He had to know. He would take her no matter what, but he had to know.

"I love you. No gratitude. No fear. No need to have a man to father our children. I love you." She lifted her hands to cup his face. "Live with me. Love with me. Any place. Anywhere." The smile that started on her lips finished on his.

"Goodbye, Solitaire," Joshua breathed as he took the mouth she offered him, took the life and the love that went with it.

Twelve

Well wife, what do you think of our family?'' Joshua whispered huskily as he slipped his arms around Leigh's slim waist. Even after eight years he still felt lucky to know this woman loved him, trusted him to share her life, her thoughts and her fears.

"I can't believe we've managed to increase to three in such a short time," Leigh murmured softly, staring out over the crowded backyard. Every time she looked at her family Leigh knew what the word miracle meant. She hadn't been blessed with just one child, but three.

Balloons, streamers and tables covered with bright cloths proclaimed the seventh birthday of Jay, the oldest of the Dancer clan. The precocious five-year-old twins, Elaine and Ellen, were holding court with the young male guests. The rest of the age-assorted guests were friends of all the children.

"Sometimes I can't believe we did it." Leigh leaned back against Joshua's chest, as always conscious of his strength and love supporting her. He had always been there. No shadow of betrayed trust darkened her eyes these days.

Joshua rested his chin on the cloud of silvery hair while he gazed at his brood. "And likely to do it again," he remarked quietly. "Only this time with a twist."

Leigh tipped her head to frown up at him. How had he known? She wasn't even sure herself. "What are you talking about? We agreed three was enough."

"But that was before you started talking about adopting a child no one wanted," he pointed out, holding her tight. The first time she had made the suggestion he had been surprised. Much as they both loved their children they still had their problems, one of them being that Leigh's time was at a premium. Now his wife was talking about adding another to their household. Bending his head, he brushed her lips with his. "We have a full house. Three children, two dogs, a turtle and, let's not forget, Mrs. McKay who keeps us organized. Add to that, Country Crafts has a new location in Memphis. You, my love, are a woman among many."

Leigh brushed a kiss over his lips, not hiding the pleasure of his compliment. "I'm glad I married you," she whispered.

"Flattery will get you anywhere you want to go," he whispered back before giving her bottom a light tap. "But only after you tell me about this child. I was never so surprised in my life when a caseworker called me, out of the blue, about adopting a little girl." He paused, then added, "No, I'll take that back. I think one other time in our life, you managed to throw me a curve."

Leigh laughed. "You mean when I told you about having twins," she teased, remembering his shock vividly.

Josh glared down at her, not meaning a bit of it. "Exactly. And look where that got me. Two o'clock feedings with one squaller while you handled the other."

"You loved it," she reminded him.

"I did and you, my lady, are stalling so give. Where and when did you hear about this child?"

Leigh was relieved that Josh knew about her errand. She had gone to the children's facility because she couldn't help being touched by the history of the poor mite they were discussing. She hadn't thought beyond that until she had seen Belinda for herself.

"From the mother of Jay's friend, Timmy," she replied, realizing Josh was waiting patiently for her answer. "She and her husband foster children, remember? They had served as an emergency shelter for this one when the authorities took her from her parents." Leigh cuddled closer in his arms. "Yesterday was an impulse I can't explain. I just had to see her. I know I should have discussed it with you. It never oc-

curred to me that the caseworker would call you."
Laying her head against his chest, she confessed, "I
wanted to cry when I saw her. Do you know she didn't
smile once the whole time I was there? It nearly killed
me."

Leigh had promised herself she wouldn't ask.
Joshua had given her so much. She had him and the
family she wanted. So much love lived in their home.
Was she being greedy by even considering another
child? The memory of the poor, bruised little face
haunted her. "Just one more child. I swear. She's
going to need medical care to repair the damage and
that's expensive. We can afford it where others can't,
even if they could handle the problems she is bound to
have. Generous as the state can be, we can do better."

"I know. Believe me, I'd like to have her, too." He
smiled at her look of surprise. "After the caseworker
called I had to see her, too."

Leigh let out a breath she hadn't even known she'd
been holding. It was going to be all right.

"Think, Leigh. Your schedule is a killer. I don't
know how you keep up with us all. Can you really
handle the demands this child is going to make? I love
you too much to let you ruin yourself in the attempt.
We're just two people. We have the family we
wanted."

Leigh met his eyes, aware of the sound of happy
children around her. Their children would never know
want or pain physically inflicted by their parents. Belinda had already known both. Leigh couldn't bear
that knowledge. Because she couldn't, the decision she

had never thought she needed to make thanks to Joshua's understanding and love, had come. For eight years she had successfully juggled being a wife, mother and business person. She could go on as she was, or give up one thing to make room for something else. She knew it and could see the same knowledge in Joshua's eyes. Belinda would have problems and would need more care and love than most children. The little girl would need the security of a full-time mother. Suddenly Leigh wanted privacy, time alone with her husband, the man she loved.

"Let's go inside. Mrs. K. can watch the party for a while." Slipping out of his arms, she caught his hand.

Joshua followed her into the study, the one haven of solitude they had from the family. Halting beside his favorite chair, he sat down and pulled Leigh into his lap. "Now give. What's going on in that beautiful head of yours. I thought I understood when I saw Belinda. Now I'm not so sure."

Leigh leaned against him, uncertain how to explain. The idea was so new. "I've been thinking about the business and us, you, me, and the kids." She hesitated, searching his face for understanding but finding only puzzlement. "I want to be a full-time mother and wife," she confessed in a rush. "I want to bake cookies, go to PTA meetings and help with homework. I want to slave over a hot stove waiting for you to come home from the office after a hard day."

Whatever he'd expected it hadn't been this, Joshua realized, momentarily stunned at her revelation. Would Leigh never stop surprising him? "But what about your business? Country Crafts III isn't even a year old yet."

"I know, but don't you see? I'm greedy. I want it all. I've had success. I know who I am and what I can do. I don't need to prove anything to myself or anyone else. I can really be what I've always wanted to be."

Joshua framed her face with his hands. Had she ever been more beautiful? She was his, all of her. The uncertainty, the need she trusted him with enough to confide, the touch of fear she shared, and the hint of pleading she probably had no idea existed in her eyes, didn't diminish the strength in her that he loved so much.

"You're sure? What about the stores?"

"I'll sell them."

"Just like that?"

"Just like that." She encircled his wrists, feeling the steady beat of his pulse beneath her palms. He was always there holding her, loving her when she needed him most.

"No regrets?"

"None." She could feel the tension invading her body as she awaited his reaction. She valued his opinion both as a husband and a businessman.

"You're going to be one wealthy woman."

"I know, and I'll need one really sharp financial wizard to keep me that way," she teased, feeling almost light-headed with his agreement. "Do you think I'm crazy?" She caught her breath at the love that shone out of his eyes.

"You're crazy all right. Crazy beautiful, generous and so loving you leave me speechless," he managed, capturing her mouth in a searing kiss that celebrated the life and the love they had created together. When he lifted his head to stare at her, they were both breathing heavily.

"I always wanted an even number of children. Of course Jay is going to be outnumbered."

"You don't mind?"

"Mind?" He hugged her close. "I always wanted to come home from the office to the little woman waiting to cool my poor overworked brow."

Relieved and excited at the same time, Leigh hugged him back. "Just don't get too carried away with the scenario. I might be home but you're going to be henpecked just like all good traditional hubbies are."

"Who cares as long as you love me as I love you," he shot back, beginning his favorite task of getting her out of her clothes.

"Always. In all ways," she breathed, reciprocating in kind. Her eyes were soft with the passion his touch never failed to create in her, this man, her love and the light of her life.

* * * * *

Silhouette Desire

COMING NEXT MONTH

#391 BETRAYED BY LOVE—Diana Palmer
Kate had loved Jacob forever, but he had always considered her off limits. She couldn't risk telling him her true feelings—but then Jacob started taking some risks of his own....

#392 RUFFLED FEATHERS—Katherine Granger
Cass was sure that Ryan's interest in her was strictly business. He was playing with her heart to get her uncle's secret recipe. But one look at Cass and Ryan knew he was playing for keeps.

#393 A LUCKY STREAK—Raye Morgan
Kelly's life was secure until she rescued gambler Cash Angeli from a gang of thugs. They were from different worlds, but together they found a lifelong lucky streak.

#394 A TASTE OF FREEDOM—Candice Adams
When Felicity met Clark, she knew immediately he was a man with a past. She was shocked when she discovered his secret, but then it was too late—he'd already stolen her heart.

#395 PLAYING WITH MATCHES—Ariel Berk
Adrienne's business was matchmaking, but she was *always* mistaken when it came to herself. When she fell for Scott she knew he must be all wrong, but Scott was determined to change her mind!

#396 TWICE IN A LIFETIME—BJ James
Stonebridge was a quiet place to recuperate for Gabe—but when Caroline fell off the roof and into his arms, rest was the last thing on his mind.

AVAILABLE NOW:

COMING NEXT MONTH

Silhouette Classics

**The best books from the past by
your favorite authors.**

The first two stories of a delightful collection . . .

#1 DREAMS OF EVENING by Kristin James

As a teenager, Erica had given Tonio Cruz all her love, body and soul,
but he betrayed and left her anyway. Ten years later, he was back in her
life, and she quickly discovered that she still wanted him. But the
situation had changed—now she had a son. A son who was very much
like his father, Tonio, the man she didn't know whether to hate—or love.

#2 INTIMATE STRANGERS by Brooke Hastings

Rachel Grant had worked hard to put the past behind her, but Jason
Wilder's novel about her shattered her veneer of confidence. When they
met, he turned her life upside down again. Rachel was shocked to
discover that Jason wasn't the unfeeling man she had imagined. Haunted
by the past, she was afraid to trust him, but he was determined to write a
new story about her—one that had to do with passion and tenderness
and love.

SCLB